CIRCLE OF
NIGHTMARES

Jodie felt something sickening inside her head. It felt as if a fist had taken hold of her brain and callously squeezed the life out of it. No longer in command of herself, her legs buckled and she crashed into the undergrowth. Ryan felt an effect like a sledgehammer inside his skull and he dropped to the ground as if he had been poleaxed. Wolfie ceased to run in a straight line. Uncontrolled, he veered off comically to the left, leaning further and further until his legs tangled hopelessly and he toppled on to his side, landing in an inelegant heap. All three of them lay unnaturally still.

Other gripping books by Malcolm Rose:

Point

CIRCLE OF NIGHTMARES

Malcolm Rose

■SCHOLASTIC

With thanks to Barbara and Colin for listening.

Scholastic Children's Books
Commonwealth House, 1–19 New Oxford Street,
London WC1A 1NU, UK
a division of Scholastic Ltd
London ~ New York ~ Toronto ~ Sydney ~ Auckland

First published in the UK by Scholastic Ltd, 1997

Copyright © Malcolm Rose, 1997

ISBN 0 590 13383 7

Typeset by TW Typesetting, Midsomer Norton, Somerset
Printed by Cox & Wyman Ltd, Reading, Berks.

10 9 8 7 6 5 4 3 2 1

The scientific content of this book is factually based. Reports released under the Freedom of Information Act in the USA testify to the reality of the project code-named Pandora.

1

The night reeked of evil. Inky clouds blotted out the stars. Only a glimmer of half-moon penetrated the gloom. Without even a hint of wind, the summer air was oppressively warm and stale. In the dormant wood the trees were as motionless as statues of the dead. The leaves had ceased to rustle. Birds and bats no longer fluttered through the dark roof of the beechwood. On the heathland, even the crickets had ceased their chirping.

One creature did venture to the edge of the murky wood and gaze stealthily over the heath. Its eyes glinted faintly as it moved its head from side to side, scanning the moor. Noiselessly, it skirted the boundary of the wood, slinking at one moment, then pausing and hanging its nose in the air to catch an intriguing scent. The animal froze, crouching when it reached the stone circle. Involuntarily, its tongue lolled and saliva dripped from its hungry mouth.

A few paces from the last line of trees, the stones had stood for five thousand years. Thirty small pillars of sandstone made a perfect circle, nearly forty metres across, like a ring of soldiers spaced four metres apart, standing silently on sentry. Just outside the ring on its eastern side, there was a larger pitted stone, over two metres high. The circle was a monument to some long-lost culture. For one night every month, it was claimed by the followers of the old ways. This night, though, there were no pagan rituals. Instead, lambs were tethered to each of the stones in the circle. Thirty innocents, all waiting, unable to scatter. They shifted restlessly as if they sensed the danger.

Leaving the shadows of the beeches, the large scruffy dog began to prowl round the ancient site at a distance. The wolfhound's grey and wiry coat concealed an unnaturally thin body. Cruelly abandoned by its owners, the wolfhound had become wild. It had reverted to its hunting instinct and it was hungry. It seemed intent on encircling its prey before pouncing. Perhaps it suspected a trap, or maybe it was simply selecting the most vulnerable victim. It was even possible that the wolfhound could not believe its luck. Coming back to the point where the heath gave way to the wood, it lay low, fixed its gaze on one particular lamb near the large stone and began to creep towards it.

The lamb lifted its face and surveyed the territory. It tilted its head quizzically and bleated twice. It did not see the predator but it knew that there was something out there. It backed away. The rope that tethered it to the stone rose off the grass.

Sneaking within a few metres of the helpless lamb, the dog suddenly sprang forward. In mid-flight, though, it pulled up. It was distracted by something that it could not see, smell, hear or feel. It stared in panic at the tall pitted stone, cowered, then turned tail and, yelping, ran back into the wood at speed, leaving behind its easy prey.

The lamb too faced the large stone. For a second, the poor creature was transfixed by fear. Then it dropped, its legs crumpling ridiculously. It was dead before its body hit the ground.

All of the nearby lambs also keeled over. Most had been stunned, a few had died. Further away, several of the terrified animals tried to bolt. Their tethers drew taut, jerked their pitiful heads and prevented escape. Across the other side of the stone circle, the lambs tottered as if they were intoxicated and several collapsed.

Five seconds after the wolfhound had fled to the safety of the wood and dashed through the gap in the fence, only nine bewildered lambs remained drunkenly on their feet.

It seemed that the circle had released a medieval, invisible and malicious energy. Newly awake in a modern world, the force had gone about its destructive ways without delay. Now, it was either exhausted or it had moved on.

A cloud drifted in front of the remaining moon, casting a shroud over the dead lambs. The night reeked of evil.

2

Jodie Hilliard's whole body jolted alarmingly. Suddenly she found herself sitting bolt upright in bed. In an instant, deep sleep had transformed into alertness. Adrenalin pumped round her body and her senses were heightened. In that state of awareness she thought that if a nocturnal rabbit rubbed a paw over its cheeks and whiskers on the other side of the valley, she'd hear it. Foolish, she knew, but sometimes in the dead of night she imagined all things were possible. She glanced at her clock. Twelve-thirty. She didn't know what had roused her so abruptly so she felt wary and anxious. Not frightened. Jodie didn't frighten easily. It was the mystery of her wakening that made her tense. Jodie liked explanations.

Soon she got her answer. The noise of the dustbin clattering on the paving stones below her window. It demolished the quiet like thunder. One of the local cats often tipped off the lid to scavenge inside but this sounded like the whole bin going over. A larger animal. Jodie groaned and got up. She parted the curtains and peered into the extraordinarily dark night. She shuddered. The moon had not surrendered completely to the brutal clouds but it was losing the battle. Down below in the garden, she could just make out the bin on its side, rubbish scattered around, and the body of a large dog. With its neck and head embedded in the bin, the foraging dog looked like it was wearing an absurd outsized hat. No doubt, it was after her dad's dinner. Jodie had cooked for herself and her father just before he'd rung to say that he was working late. She banged on her bedroom window and the dog, an Irish wolfhound she thought, hit its thick skull on the inside of the bin and then extracted it quickly. It looked around apprehensively and Jodie knocked on the window again. The nervous hound could not locate the source of the noise but it had had enough. Hurriedly, it grabbed the remains of the meat in its teeth and sprang away.

"I don't know why its owners don't look after it and feed it properly," she mumbled to herself. She'd have to clear up the intruder's mess in the morning. She turned away from the window. With both hands, she ruffled her short black hair. The house was quiet. She wondered if her dad had returned so she tiptoed along the landing without turning on the lights and squinted into his room. The bed was unruffled and unoccupied. Jodie crept downstairs. None of the lamps were on and the rooms were devoid of life. "Past midnight," she whispered. "That's what I call working late."

She was well aware that, in the village, her father was known as the mad professor. She understood why. Eleven months ago, he'd come to live in Greenwood End with his only daughter and without a wife. Suspicious. He worked in the clandestine Government laboratory at the head of the valley. Secretive. He wouldn't talk much about his work and, even if he did, few would understand his branch of physics. Incomprehensible. And he worked at all sorts of strange hours. Crazy. But he wasn't mad. Not really. Just … single-minded. He was a workaholic, sometimes so intent on a target that he didn't notice how much he neglected Jodie. Selfish and uncaring. But he wasn't. Not really. Just … a bit divorced from reality. A bit damaged. He neglected himself, as well.

Jodie plonked herself into a chair with a wry grin. She didn't mind being the daughter of a mad professor but she wished that the locals weren't so wary of him and anything to do with him and the Research Station. Then she might not feel so isolated from life in Greenwood End. Apart from Leah, the villagers shunned Jodie and her mad professor father. Besides, he wasn't mad – and he wasn't yet a professor but a doctor of physics. Since Jodie's mum died, physics had taken over his life. When he could talk about his work with Jodie, he did so with a childlike glee and enthusiasm. At least Jodie could understand him. She was taking physics, maths and computing at a sixth-form college in High Wycombe and everyone knew that, next summer holiday, she'd be about to embark on an electronics course at university.

3

The wolfhound licked his lips. The morsels from the dustbin had whetted his appetite, rather than satisfied it. He lifted his muzzle and sniffed the air. He caught the scent of food. It drifted on the still air along with the stale whiff of something that his owner used to drink. He loped towards the source of the aroma, still intent on scrounging an ample meal.

At one side of the building there was a road. The dog had once been hurt on a road, so he avoided it. At the back of the property, there were stacked barrels and crates of empty bottles. They gave off a musty, unappealing stench. The tantalizing smell of food came from inside the building itself. Unable to resist its allure, he padded warily up to the back door. It was slightly open and inside a light was on in one of the rooms. The voice of a single human floated down the hallway. "Show us what you need."

The nervous dog crouched down, ready for flight or fight, but there was no further noise. He raised his nose and sampled the air again. There may have been only one voice but he detected odours from several human beings. Some natural smells, some that they got from bottles and cans. The more attractive trail led to a darkened room on his left.

Suddenly, the same human called out again. "Show us what you want," it implored.

The wolfhound pushed open the door with his snout and slipped inside. He recognized the room by its smells as the place where humans prepared meals. This, though, was much larger than his owner's kitchen. In the bin, there were untold delights. Immediately, he pushed his head into it and sunk his teeth into vegetable peelings, scraps of cooked meat and raw meat on the bone. He bolted down as much as he could, as quickly as he could.

He was so engrossed, devouring the remnants that the humans had rejected, that he didn't hear one of them approach. Behind him, a female let out a screech. The wolfhound spun round in fright. She was blocking the door.

Within a few seconds, four men joined her and stared menacingly at him. The largest of the men exclaimed, "It's the sign." He was the one who had spoken before and he was wearing an old black gown with crimson embroidery and a putrid smell that the dog did not recognize.

One of the others added, "No collar. He's a stray. Perfect."

"I told you we'd get a message at the end of the midnight meeting."

"A dog. Exactly what you'd expect in a place called The Olde Spotted Dog."

"Except he's no Dalmatian."

"No matter," said the one with the moth-eaten cloak. "He's the sign."

The wolfhound crouched, bared his teeth and snarled as the leader approached him with his hand extended.

"Watch out," another of the humans warned. "He's going to make a dash for it!"

"He might be vicious."

The first man said to the dog, "Are you hungry? I can give you a great big beefy bone. Then you won't run, will you?"

The dog was too terrified and flustered to wait to find out what the man was going to do. He reacted in the only way he knew. He rocked back on his haunches and emitted a low growl that stopped the humans in their tracks.

"I told you. Careful. He's big and powerful."

The wolfhound leapt forward and snapped at the

man's hand. As the human yelled in pain and clutched his bleeding hand, the dog charged out of the room, brushing past the others who lifted up their arms so that he would not bite them.

"Get him!" the man in the gown shouted.

The dog hurtled out of the back door and into the night. Behind him one of the humans reported, "No chance. He's fast and it's too dark."

"All right," the first replied. "He won't go far. Not now he knows there's food here. We'll bait a trap with food and catch him next time. There's nine days before we have to have him."

The Irish wolfhound made for the cover of the wood as quickly as he could. Anywhere away from people. Even if he'd nearly been captured in the village, it was worth it because he had a full belly.

High above him, the clouds parted at last and let the moon peep through. Somehow, with its reappearance, the night became normal again. The customary sounds resumed. Scratching and scrabbling, fluttering, calling, chirping. With the end of the midnight gathering, the evil was suspended.

4

Still in the chair, Jodie drifted. She thought of her mother, their move to the Buckinghamshire countryside last September so that her dad could take the place of the previous scientist who had committed suicide, and the lad she'd met that afternoon. Ryan. She hoped he didn't turn out to be another wolfhound because she thought she quite liked him.

When she next jerked awake, she recognized the cause straightaway. The light was on and her dad was standing in front of her, gazing fondly at his daughter and smiling.

"Sorry," he mumbled gently. "I was just trying to decide if I'm still capable of carrying you up to bed without disturbing you – like I used to when you were little. I think not."

She rubbed her eyes. "Late," she moaned, still drowsy.

"Yeah. Lots of work to get done. Couldn't wait till morning, I'm afraid. Anyway," he whispered, "why aren't *you* in bed?"

"Werewolves kept me awake," Jodie mumbled.

"It's not a full moon. Must be mistaken. Perhaps it was the village ghost."

Jodie yawned and stretched. Emerging from her stupor like a dozy tortoise from hibernation, she said, "Yeah. Either that or a stray wolfhound help-ing itself to your dinner out of the dustbin."

"Ah, yes. Sorry about that. I grabbed a sandwich at work."

Much more attentive now, she checked, "A sand-wich? Are you sure?" She sounded like a mother. At seventeen, she was mother to a forty-year-old!

"Well, OK, I didn't," her dad confessed. "But I wasn't hungry."

"Dad! You're thin enough as it is. You've got to eat properly." She sighed. "Do you want something now?" She looked at her watch and was surprised to see that it was one twenty-five.

"Too late for a midnight feast," he replied. "Let's go to bed now. I'll get a big breakfast in the morn-ing," he declared.

Used to broken pledges, Jodie looked at him distrustfully.

"Promise," he swore, ushering her back upstairs.

As he waved her towards the stairs, Jodie noticed a bandage round his right hand. Concerned, she asked, "What have you done to your hand?"

"It's nothing," he replied. "An accident. I smashed some glassware at work and a piece of the glass bit me. The nurse took care of it."

Jodie sighed but did not castigate her beleaguered dad further.

The lorry reversed up to the outbuilding and came to a halt with a hiss of its air brakes and a clanking of milk churns. The driver jumped down from his cabin and joined the farmer who was standing, arms akimbo, at the edge of this field.

"Well, I'll be damned," the driver said.

The farmer glanced at him. "What do you make of that, then?"

They were looking at two fully grown swans sitting in untidy heaps among the cattle.

"What are they doing there?" asked the dairy driver.

"Search me," the farmer answered. "They belong on the pond. On the other side of the house. Must have crash-landed like a couple of them Concordes in the night. Don't know why they came down so wide of the mark. Never happened before."

"Are they hurt?"

"Imagine so. I can't get close enough to see. They start their hissing as soon as I go near. They don't seem to be going anywhere. They probably hit the ground and tumbled quite a bit. Bet something's broken."

"Strange. I suppose it means someone's been up to tricks again."

"Could be."

The farmer looked wistfully in the direction of the Research Station on the other side of the road while the driver peered across the fields to the village and The Olde Spotted Dog.

"I'd better call the vet."

With a wry smile, the driver responded, "Yes. Simon'll know all about it, if anyone does."

"Ah well. Best get the churns loaded. One fewer today. Yield's down again, I'm afraid. Something's bothering them," he said, nodding towards his cows. "Perhaps I'll get Simon to look at the herd while he's here. See what he thinks."

Jodie didn't want a cooked breakfast but she forced herself into it so as to keep her dad company. If she'd opted for cereal and toast, he would have found an excuse to eat the same. So, it had to be unfancied mushrooms, sausage and tomatoes to ensure that her preoccupied father ate something substantial that day. After he left for work, Jodie cleaned up the kitchen, and then the garden where the dog had neglected its table manners. She replaced the bin lid and perched a brick on top of it.

As she did so, she came to a decision about the wolfhound.

Jodie strolled into the village that nestled snugly into the Chiltern hillside. It was a gorgeous day so she wore shorts and T-shirt. At the quiet crossroads, she nodded towards Ben Godwin, the landlord of The Olde Spotted Dog, who was sweating profusely over a delivery of barrels of beer. As always, he ignored her. He was a big, bearded man and he reminded Jodie of a rugged fisherman or a less-than-jolly Father Christmas. Strangely, he was wearing gloves – to protect his hands from splinters of wood, Jodie presumed. Ben was definitely one of the people who regarded her father as a mad scientist, but then he was decidedly peculiar himself. And it wasn't just his stupid, extravagant moustache. Jodie could never quite articulate her qualms about him and his cronies who congregated in the pub, but they were odd. The antiquated inn was not popular with tourists. It should have been a real attraction because it looked very quaint, but the regulars were hardly welcoming. When strangers walked in, the place went quiet as if an atrocity had just been committed. The murmur of the clan would gradually return and the tourists would get served politely but without warmth.

Outside one of the houses, a small girl, perhaps nine years old, was dissolving in tears. Jodie squatted down in front of her and said gently, "What's your name?"

"Kelly." The girl continued to sob and choke.

"What's the problem?" Jodie asked, kindly. "Perhaps I can help."

"You can't," Kelly cried. "It's Mummy and Daddy. They're sending Suki away. They say she's having too many kittens." She wiped her mouth and added, "They say I can keep one of her kittens but it won't be the same as having Suki."

From inside the house a sharp paternal voice called, "Kelly! Come away. I want you in here – now!"

Jodie thought that Kelly's parents were being heavy-handed and heartless towards their daughter but, to Kelly, she said, "Never mind. I bet that kitten'll turn out to be a really great pet." She watched the pitiful girl amble back inside, exaggerating the grief to show her parents the devastation that they had caused.

In the village store, two women were clustered round Marissa Birkby at the check-out. They looked like three witches and they were saying, "Poor old Eleanor. She's still hankering after a baby. Her and Dave have been trying for years but there's no sign…" When they saw Jodie, they stopped their conversation and dispersed. Jodie smiled. It was a pity, she thought, that Eleanor couldn't have a little of what Suki the cat had got in apparent abundance. Jodie filled her basket with provisions and took them to one of the three witches – the old-fashioned

Marissa at the old-fashioned till. Electronic tagging had not yet reached Greenwood End. It threatened never to do so. Laboriously, Marissa picked up each item and recorded its price. When she got to one tin, she held it out and said, "What's this?" Her demanding tone suggested that Jodie had no right to want it.

Jodie's eyebrows rose. "It's dog food," she said curtly.

"I can see that. But you don't have…"

"We might acquire one," Jodie stated, determined not to explain her purchase because she didn't take kindly to Marissa's attitude. Besides, the storekeeper's job was to sell, not to question. Jodie grasped the tin of dog food firmly, placed it in her bag and returned Marissa's suspicious stare.

"That dad of yours," Marissa enquired, "is he still up the road at the Research Station?" She frowned as she pronounced the name of the laboratory. She posed the same question every time that Jodie went into the shop. Rather like some people always comment on the weather, Marissa always asked about Jodie's father.

"Yes," Jodie answered. "He's still there. Still doing fine, thank you."

Marissa cackled, "Last two before him, they both killed themselves, you know. Or so they say."

Two? Jodie knew only about her dad's immediate predecessor. "Who's *they*?"

"Oh, you know. The papers and things."

"Do you know any different?" Jodie prompted. It was virtually a challenge.

"Me?" Marissa exclaimed. She snorted. "No. That's science and stuff up there. I don't know anything about that. All I know is they fiddle about with nature. No good'll come of it. You mark my words. And tell your father. You can try the patience of nature too much. Bad news comes in threes."

Jodie lifted up her bag and shook her head. She murmured, "Thanks." Really, she wanted to tell Marissa not to be such a superstitious fool but instead she hurried out of the store and back home.

In vacations, when her dad was out at work, Jodie would keep herself busy. Although she'd failed to get a part-time job in the village – after almost a year in Greenwood End she was still considered an outsider – she still had her computer and electronics workshop. It had been set up first by her father but was now ruled by Jodie. She surrounded herself with gadgets like a squirrel hoarding nuts from the beech trees. Turning on her scanner, she tapped in a frequency of 927.2 MHz and played with the fine tuning. Almost immediately someone's mobile telephone conversation filled the small room. "I'm sorry. I got caught up in an accident on the M40. I should be with you about half an hour late. Can I still see you or will I have to make another appointment?" There were a few seconds of silence as the caller listened to the reply. "Good," the male voice said in a smarmy tone. "Sorry to inconvenience you, but I'm sure you'll find it worth your while to rearrange your schedule. I think you'll be very impressed with the specifications of our new RFR generator. The R402A." The voice faded and died as the mobile phone frequency changed automatically because its user was moving. If it had been a riveting conversation, she would have tried to lock on to it with her hand-held sniffer. She would have also tried to capture both sides of the exchange by scanning the local cellnet frequencies. Stuck out in the wilds, there weren't that many to test – only about 20 – so usually she could record a complete conversation. She'd never stumbled upon a conversation involving members of the Royal family, as far as she knew, but she'd enjoyed eaves-dropping on some juicy calls. She'd once heard her MP arranging a meeting with a woman while his wife was at work. The woman sounded young and flirtatious. In her mind, Jodie had constructed an image of the female caller, solely on the basis of her voice and her name. She wondered if her perception was anywhere near reality. She'd hit upon a drugs deal once – arranged by mobile phone. Crazy to discuss such things on mobile phones, really, because it's so easy to listen in. Police frequencies were always interesting. A car chase was best. The officers would get so irate when they lost someone they were chasing. The language was impressively graphic. Listening to aircraft traffic and satellite transmissions was also revealing for someone as curious and nosy as Jodie. So much more exciting than the radio. It was a good giggle.

She'd just got absorbed in the Internet when the doorbell rang. Jodie glanced at her watch and mumbled to herself, "Leah."

At the start of the school year, when Jodie was new to the village, she found herself next to Leah waiting for the same bus into High Wycombe to go to the same college. When Jodie tried a smile, Leah didn't look the other way. In a distrustful village, Jodie had to clutch at the merest straw of friendship so she started a tentative conversation. Other than the journey and the college, they had little in common. Jodie lapped up an education in science like a thirsty cat with a bowlful of cream. Leah was taking a couple of humanities A-levels reluctantly. Really, she was too scatterbrained for academic life, but there weren't any jobs so she'd decided to stay on at school. Always on a diet, Leah groomed, manicured and adorned herself for maximum effect. Jodie was naturally pretty but attached no importance to her looks so she didn't waste time on decoration. The girls were very different and mutual curiosity rather than affection kept them together.

"What you doing?" asked Leah.

"Making us a coffee?" Jodie proposed.

"Why not? But, I mean, what are you doing really?"

"Guess."

"Playing with the computer?"

Jodie nodded. "Of course. I'll show you. I've found something really disgusting." She put the kettle on and commented, "I know what *you've* been doing."

"What?"

Jodie touched her own nose and nodded towards Leah's. "Sunbathing." Leah's nose shone bright red like a beacon. Either side of the straps of her skimpy top, her shoulders were as pink as prawns. "It's not good for you, you know. All that ultraviolet. Skin cancer beckons."

"I know, but… It's nice to be out in the sun. I mean, we don't get that much. You've got to make the most of it."

"Have you?" Jodie replied. "Sunscreen. That's what you need."

Taking care not to spill coffee on to the keyboard, Jodie showed Leah her discovery. A new virtual world. "It's a game from Japan. You're offered virtual friendships and even virtual love affairs. See? A man picks a mate from these ten women and then strikes up a relationship with her. He chooses her figure, clothes, hobbies, everything, and then 'meets' her and 'raises' her. It says the relationship develops just like in real life. And, of course, it goes as far as the man wants. Real life!" Jodie scorned. "In real life, she'd tell him to sod off."

"What's disgusting about it?" Leah asked naively.

"Well, can't you see it's for sad, inadequate blokes who can't cope with reality? Don't you think, if they try real life after practising with this, they'll believe they own a girlfriend and dictate everything?"

"I don't know," Leah replied disinterestedly. She picked up Jodie's RF sniffer and started to fiddle with it. "But you're a fine one to talk about real life. I mean, cutting yourself off in here."

"Thanks, Leah!" Playfully, Jodie slapped her friend's hand, took the sniffer from her and put it back safely on the desk.

"I didn't mean to be... Don't get me wrong. I don't think you're sad or inadequate. I just reckon you've shut yourself off a bit. No sunbathing. No boys."

"If this is what boys get reared on, I'm better off out of it," Jodie complained. "Anyway, that reminds me. I meant to ask you. What do you know about a lad called Ryan?"

"Ryan Aplin!" Leah exploded. "Get in the queue! Why?"

"Oh, we bumped into each other yesterday. Almost literally – outside The Olde Spotted Dog. I'm seeing him this evening."

Leah's mouth opened but it took a while for the stunned words to emerge. "This evening? You lucky thing! Perhaps you're coming out of your shell after all."

"What's he like, though? Is he … safe? You know."

"You'll be all right. I mean, compared to some, he's a saint. He actually talks, he doesn't just say his rehearsed lines, shuffle about a bit nervously and then grab. Nineteen, hunky, cute, witty, no spots. Works at Hughenden Manor – so he's not short of cash. Need I go on?"

"How long's he lived here?"

Leah exhaled noisily as she thought. "Just about for ever. His family moved here – from Scotland, I think – when he was a baby. Long enough to be pillars of the community. The real natives, though, the old folk, still think of the Aplins as newcomers – outsiders, like you. I mean, you don't count if you haven't got at least three generations in the parish register. But Ryan's OK. Even fancies himself as a local historian. He's always been into old books, records, old wives' tales, rumours. Consumes it all. Now he knows more than those folk with ancestors in the parish register." She giggled at a memory and then explained to Jodie, "At secondary school, everyone used him as the oracle for anything we had to write about Buckinghamshire. Well, the girls did anyway."

"Doesn't sound like he'd need Woman Maker games from Japan," Jodie concluded with a smile.

"Where are you seeing him?" asked an excited Leah.

"That would be telling," Jodie said, wagging her finger at her friend. "I'm not having you hiding behind the nearest bush, eavesdropping."

"Oh, yeah. Like you don't approve of eavesdropping!" Leah glanced at Jodie's cluttered electronic haven and concluded, "Only bad girls listen in to other people's private chats."

Jodie chuckled. "That's different. Anyway," she added, "something else I was going to ask you. Have you seen a scrawny Irish wolfhound around the village? Know anything about it?"

The humour of their banter drained from Leah's face. "Wolfhound?" She frowned and then looked at the floor before answering, "Er... No. Why?"

5

Jodie scraped out half of the unappetizing dog food into an old dish. Then she hesitated before adding the rest of the smelly gel into the bowl, muttering, "Well, he is a big dog." She left the offering by the dustbin. That way, she hoped to avoid another mammoth, messy clean-up operation in the morning. Besides, she liked dogs. It was dog *owners* who would often make her angry.

Ryan was already waiting at the village green. He'd pulled his car partly on to the grass and was leaning on the open passenger's door. "Hi!" he said brightly, apparently delighted that he hadn't been stood up.

Jodie nodded. "Hello."

"Jump in," he chirped, turning on the charm and holding the door open for her.

"Where do you think we're going?" she asked, with a trace of petulance in her voice.

"There's a nice place in High Wycombe. We'll grab a meal and, if you want, go on to a club. OK?"

Jodie didn't like to be left out of the planning. She wanted to be part of the decisions. "Let's just stick with the meal. Clubs aren't really me."

Ryan grinned. "Good. I only offered because it's the done thing," he confessed. "Thought you might expect it – so I volunteered. I'd rather go to a nice pub. Maybe with live folk music? That's more me."

"Mmm." Jodie did not return his smile. "Not exactly my idea of a good time," she murmured. In her usual forthright manner, she added, "As I said, let's leave it at a meal. We might be sick of the sight of each other before the end of the first course."

Ryan chuckled pleasantly. "Let's hope not." He started the car and pulled away. He didn't show off by leaving some rubber in the road and flinging Jodie's head on to the rest.

"Don't you work at Hughenden Manor?" Jodie enquired.

"Home of Benjamin Disraeli. Died in 1881. His grave's in the churchyard, his ghost's at the foot of the cellar stairs – and sometimes on the upper floors."

"You don't believe that sort of stuff, do you?"

"Depends who I'm speaking to," Ryan answered. "I do tours round the house. That's part of my job.

If I want to keep it, I need to keep the visitors coming in through the door. People like haunted houses so I wouldn't want to disappoint them. They love to hear about the odd brush with a dead Prime Minister. All part of the rich culture and heritage of the area. It's called romance."

Jodie smirked. "It's also called deceit."

"Oh, the tourists don't mind being deceived when there's no harm in it. Besides, over the years, quite a few people swear they *have* seen or heard his ghost. Either way, Disraeli's more lively than our current Prime Minister – even if he is dead."

Jodie *did* believe in ghosts. Not the sort that floated through old houses, rattling chains, creaking doors and holding their heads in ludicrous positions. She knew that it was still possible to be haunted by the death of someone close.

As Ryan drove past the guarded entrance to the Research Station with its stark wire fence, spikes and ominous barrier, Jodie grimaced and twisted in her seat to watch a lorry at the gate.

"What's up?" Ryan queried.

"Nothing. Just… I don't know why they're having lambs delivered."

Ryan looked in his rear-view mirror. "Perhaps they're not," he ventured. "Perhaps the driver's stopped to ask the way."

"Unlikely."

"Oh, yes. It's your old man, isn't it? He works

there," Ryan remarked. "Why don't you ask him?"

"Most of it's hush-hush. He doesn't say much about it."

Ryan glanced at his passenger and said, "That's why the folks round here make up all sorts of rumours about suicides and mad professors, you know. When they don't understand something, they feel threatened. So they make up things for themselves. Probably much worse than the truth, but at least they can believe in their own theories – no matter how outlandish. Crazy ideas are better than mysterious nothing. Then it's not so scary." He looked sideways again to check if he'd upset her but she was nodding knowingly.

"Sounds like you're excluding yourself. You're not one of those who calls my dad the mad professor and who's scared of the Research Station?"

Ryan paused before replying. "Not scared, no. But when the Research Station first came here, when I was but a tot, they weren't exactly ... *sensitive* to the local people's views. The people here have long traditions, you know. Some of the land the Research Station took over is important to them. Not very different from the white settlers taking over the Aborigines' hunting grounds and sacred sites in Australia. Recipe for resentment. I can understand why people who work at the Research Station are sometimes called cuckoos."

"Cuckoos? I haven't heard that one."

"They've taken over the villagers' nest. There's plenty of folk in Greenwood End who'd love to get rid of the Research Station. To tell you the truth, I ... er ... can't say I blame them, if you don't mind me saying so."

Jodie didn't reply but she appreciated his honesty.

"Anyway," Ryan said, eager to change the subject, "would Mexican suit you?"

Jodie might have suggested a different meal, just so she could impose her own will on the evening, but she loved Mexican food. "That'd be fine." She nearly added that, next time, he should consult her first, but she didn't want to raise his expectations – or her own. She didn't know if there would be a next time. Not until she'd come to a verdict on him. Still, the early evidence seemed positive and promising.

Over the meal, Ryan talked about himself and his family and asked all about Jodie. He even succeeded in looking interested as she told him at length about the attractions of the Internet, hacking, listening to other people's cellnet calls, digital sound, and the rest of it. Keeping her voice down, she added enthusiastically, "There's the art of playing back messages left on other people's answering machines as well. Easy, once you've cracked the code. And I can intercept fax messages. I've adapted my fax-modem and computer to decode faxes. It's only a matter of suppressing the supervisory signals that fax machines exchange between themselves and what's left is the message."

"I'll take your word for it," Ryan muttered, bewildered but impressed by her knowledge, cunning and cheek. "Sounds fun. You already know I'm all in favour of reducing secrecy. You ... er ... must show me all this gadgetry some time."

Jodie looked into his eyes briefly and murmured, "Maybe." It was the closest that Ryan came to suggesting a visit to her house.

Even when he drove her home and parked the car outside, he left the engine running, didn't prompt for an invitation to go inside, and didn't try anything prematurely. He just thanked her and told her that he'd enjoyed the evening. "Next time," he said hopefully, "you should chose what we do. You do want to go out again, don't you?"

Jodie hesitated for effect. She'd enjoyed the evening too and knew perfectly well that she wanted to see him again. She got out of the car and then, leaning on it, bent down. "Why not?" she said, across the front seats. "If you don't mind being seen with a cuckoo, you could give me a call tomorrow."

Ryan smiled as if he meant it. "Will do!"

Before she went into the empty house, Jodie padded to the back and into the garden. She crept quietly towards the dustbin. And there he was. Caught in the act. Noisily chomping his way through the meal. Jodie squatted down and watched the dog for a few seconds and then whispered, "Hey, boy!"

The wolfhound looked up and froze.

"Don't be daft," Jodie said softly. "I put it out for you," she informed him, "so I'm not going to hurt you, am I? Even if I could. You're more likely to hurt me." Still crouching, she edged towards him.

The dog emitted a half-hearted growl and backed off.

Jodie took the bowl in her hand and held out the rest of the food towards him. "Come on," she said. "Free gift."

The unkempt hound put his head on one side and watched Jodie with curiosity but he didn't approach. He didn't look frightened either.

She put the dish down again. "Oh, you look ferocious but you're nothing but a big coward. A softie. A stupid one at that." She stood up and immediately the wolfhound took two more steps back. "Wolfie," Jodie announced. "That's what I'll call you. What else? Wolfie. You remember that," she said to him. "It's your name. I don't know what you were before but you're Wolfie now. I'll get you some more grub for tomorrow. Different flavour, perhaps." She walked away. When she looked back from the gate, she saw that Wolfie had returned to the bowl and was eagerly finishing the food.

Jodie went to bed happy. She wished that her dad

was home so she could ask him a couple of questions but otherwise she was content. In one day she was halfway to taming both Ryan and Wolfie. One meal each and they were almost eating out of her hand.

In The Olde Spotted Dog there was a short dingy hallway that linked Ben Godwin's living quarters to the bars. On either side of the corridor, in niches hollowed into its walls, there were small pottery urns. Each recess contained one of the vessels. After hours, a small group of villagers waited at the end of the hallway for the appearance of a starved wolfhound. They'd placed a bone in the shed near the back door. Tugging on a strategically placed string, they would slam the door shut as soon as the dog went inside. But they waited in vain. Their time, energy and ingenuity were wasted. The dog had had its fill elsewhere.

"There's no point trying this again," one of them grumbled as the grandfather clock in a room behind them chimed once. "We know where he's getting his food."

"The cuckoo's house."

Menacingly, the leader decided, "We'll have to change our tactics."

Mornings did not become Dr Hilliard. Never at his best in the early hours, he looked as scruffy as Wolfie and he said very little. Like a vampire, he was more of a late-night person. Over breakfast, Jodie said to him, "You never told me *two* scientists at the Research Station had killed themselves."

"Didn't I?" he replied, as if it had merely slipped his mind. "I wasn't trying to hide anything. Just didn't seem necessary. Anyway, I didn't know about that either till recently." He spooned more cereal into his mouth. He wasn't being very talkative but that was normal.

To goad more from him, Jodie said, "One suicide is a bit careless, two is downright suspicious." She was worried for her dad because it was possible that the work in the laboratory had driven them to despair.

"Jodie," her father began, wiping a fragment of bran flake from his lip, "I don't think there's anything underhand going on. The first one was a depressive, I'm told, and the second was under a bit too much stress. Couldn't cope. Actually, it's not certain the first was a suicide anyway. His car crashed at high speed into a tree, apparently. Could have been an accident. The coroner called it suicide because of the known depression and because there was nothing wrong with the car."

Not exactly reassuring. Besides, it was also possible that some of the villagers were so keen to oust the laboratory that they'd gone to extremes and made it look like suicide. Immediately, Jodie dismissed the fanciful idea and told herself not to be ridiculous. Sleepy English villages just weren't like that.

"Now," her father concluded with a forced smile, "am I going to get the rest of my breakfast in peace – without an interrogation?"

"Nope."

Jodie's dad put down his knife and muttered, "What else?" He picked up his mug of coffee.

"Do you do any work with sheep?"

For a moment, he frowned but then he grinned. "I'm a physicist, Jodie, not a farmer, or a maker of woolly hats."

"So why did I see a delivery of sheep to the Station yesterday? Maybe other animals as well. I couldn't see."

"Have you been carrying out surveillance on our fine premises, young lady?" asked her dad, unable to take the matter seriously. "Some big strong men with black balaclavas will burst in and take you away if you have."

"Mmm. Sounds promising," she quipped. Then she became serious again. "I just happened to see it when I went past with ... a boy."

"It's our biologists," her dad explained, looking at his watch. "But don't tell anyone. We'll have animal liberation people throwing themselves in front of our cars if they find out."

"What sort of experiments do they do?" she asked, with a look of distaste on her face.

"You don't want to know. But they're not killed. Or sacrificed, as biologists put it rather dramatically. They're well looked after," he answered, trying to end the difficult conversation. "You know what I think? I think you're trying to stop me asking about … that boy. What's his name? Who is he?"

Jodie was unsure of herself. Her father had become protective ever since her mother died. More than that, he'd become almost neurotic about her safety while he disregarded his own. He was apprehensive about any natives of Greenwood End who showed an interest in her because he was aware of the hostility towards newcomers. It had even taken him an age to accept Leah. Jodie could understand his concern – his insecurity – but she refused to be a hermit to satisfy him that she was safe. "He's called Ryan Aplin," she replied.

Her father's face creased. "Haven't I heard of the Aplin family?"

Jodie shrugged. "I don't know. Have you?"

"I think … I'm not sure. Perhaps not. Anyway, is he, you know, good to you?"

Jodie nodded. "He's fine, Dad. Nice. Leah says he's nice, as well."

"OK." He stood up, put his hand on her shoulder and squeezed. "I'm pleased for you. Just be careful, Jodie. You know there's a lot of ill-feeling in the village. You've got to consider the motives of anyone who tries to make friends with you. But if it feels right to you, then you've got my support – and so's he, I suppose." He exhaled and then added, "I'm late. I'll have to get moving. OK?"

Jodie tapped his hand on her shoulder. "Thanks, Dad. I'll watch my step. But you know I can look after myself."

Her father smiled ruefully. "Yes. That's one thing you've always been able to do. When I couldn't give you the attention you deserved, you always managed to get along. I think in many ways you've coped with all the changes, with your mum dying, a lot better than me." He strode off before Jodie could reply.

At times like these, when he lingered on his wife's horrible death, he reminded Jodie of a ball of string that had once been completely unravelled and deranged. In time, someone had rewound the tangled mess into a ball but it had never regained its original order. Now, the ball of string was whole but chaotic – and likely to come undone at any moment.

6

The air was alive with waves. Radiowaves, infrared, visible, ultraviolet, gamma rays. A tangled hotchpotch of frequencies. And they had the impertinence to invade everywhere. Travelling at 300 million metres per second. Some were sensed by humans, some not. Some were harmless to humans. Some harmful. But they were there to be intercepted, captured and decoded just as a mountain was there to be climbed by those who relished the challenge.

After Jodie bought a few more cans of dog food in the village but before she'd settled to a morning of sampling the inaudible and invisible messages that pervaded Greenwood End, the ringing of the telephone vibrated the air. Eagerly, she picked up the receiver and said, "Hello?" She was taken aback because it was Leah's greeting that sounded in her ear. "Oh!" she said. "Hi, Leah."

"You almost sound disappointed. Who were you expecting to call?"

"No one," she fibbed. "I was just … thinking about a computer program. You took me by surprise."

"How did it go?" Leah squawked. She was bursting with curiosity.

To keep her waiting, to tease her, Jodie played dumb. "How did what go? The computer program?"

"You know! *Ryan*."

"Oh, yes. It was all right."

"All right! Is that all you've got to say?"

"We had a meal in High Wycombe. Good food. And, yes, he was quite nice as well."

"Quite nice! Is that all? I mean, what did he say? What did you say to him? Did he come over all romantic? Are you seeing him again?"

Jodie paused. "Calm down, Leah. If I remember all those questions, the answers are an awful lot, quite a lot, no, and yes. In that order. I think."

Leah was confused. "But you *are* seeing him again?"

"I think so."

"You're so cool about it!" Leah observed, probably enviously.

"I take things a step at a time, that's all," Jodie

explained. "No point getting heated about something if a big disappointment's waiting just around the corner."

"All right," Leah replied. "But tell me what happens, won't you?"

"I'll pin updates to the village cross," Jodie said.

"By the way," Leah reported, "I think I saw that scrawny wolfhound you mentioned. Have you seen it again?"

"Yeah. Wolfie. That's what I've called him. He's becoming my chum, I think. Gave him a bit of food last night."

"Be careful, Jodie," Leah said enigmatically.

"Why?"

"Because… Well, you never know with strays. I mean, he might turn nasty."

When, eventually, Ryan called her, she arranged to meet him on the next day when he had the afternoon off work. She said, "There's a stamp collectors' fair on in Reading. I thought we could go to that."

"Stamp collecting?" Ryan exclaimed. Then he continued, "Er … yes. OK. You didn't tell me you collect stamps."

"I don't," she replied, laughing. "Just testing. I thought if you'd agree to put up with a stamp fair, you must be… Anyway, you passed the test. Let's go to the sports centre in Wycombe. I fancy some table tennis, squash or snooker. Is that all right with you?"

"Yeah. I like table tennis, even though I'm no good. You can slaughter me. Snooker or squash... Well, you won't stand a chance."

"Huh. Chickens and counting them too early come to mind."

After making the arrangements, Jodie gave her full attention to her listening post. But the only people calling each other were innocently ordering a dial-a-curry, asking after a parent's hay fever, reporting the breakdown of a car, contributing a bigoted opinion to a radio phone-in. All rather tedious. Even the police weren't chasing anything exciting. Instead, Jodie's mind turned to her dad's work. She was still worried by it. She could not accept that two suicides by scientists at the same research establishment were merely an unhappy coincidence. If her dad was not concerned for himself, she'd have to be concerned on his behalf. She booted her computer and began the long and laborious task of hacking into the Research Station.

Lights out, Jodie sat in her bedroom and surveyed the garden, the dark wood beyond, and the clear sky. With each night, more of the electromagnetic radiation from the sun was reflected towards Greenwood End by the moon which seemed to swell with warmth. Perversely, it was when the moon was full, bathed in a beautiful glow, that evil was said to be at its height. To Jodie, it didn't make sense.

First, Wolfie appeared from the trees as a slender silhouette. The blot on the lawn moved slowly and warily. If she hadn't known better, Jodie could have interpreted the black shadowy figure as a threat. Quietly, she rose and slunk downstairs. In the kitchen, she grabbed the bowl, already full of dog food, and then slipped out through the back door.

The dog was sniffing the paving stones near the dustbin. Jodie got the impression that he was disappointed until his nose caught the smell of the food in her hand. Again, his head tipped to one side as he gazed at her.

"Hello, Wolfie," she whispered. "I didn't forget you. Here it is." She held out the dish.

This time the dog did not back off. His eyes flicked between Jodie's face and the bowl of food as if he were trying to weigh his distrust against his hunger.

Jodie placed the bowl on the ground midway between them and then sat back to watch. "You don't understand charity and friendliness much, do you, Wolfie?"

The dog's paws were rooted to the spot but he strained forward as far as he dared, stretching his neck to sniff at the enticing food.

Jodie giggled. "You daft dog. You'll fall in it if you're not careful."

His nose twitched, his lips opened. He was like a small boy, tempted beyond endurance by an opened bar of chocolate that he'd been told not to eat. With a final glance at Jodie, he stepped forward and sank his snout into the soft meat. Between mouthfuls, he kept watch on the woman who had provided the meal.

"My, you are hungry," Jodie said gently. Reminding herself of a fairy tale, she added, "My, what big teeth you've got."

Wolfie didn't reply. He wasn't going to live up to his name. He was quite tame, really.

Suddenly, both Wolfie and Jodie looked towards the edge of the murky wood. They had both heard the same noise. After a few seconds, Wolfie returned to his meal, but Jodie stood up. She took a couple of steps towards the end of the lawn and called, "Who's there?" She was sure that she'd heard someone stumbling in the gloom. There was no reply, though. She left Wolfie and nipped back inside. When she came back out, she was carrying a large torch and she directed its powerful beam of visible light towards the trees. When she was small, she'd play the beam into the sky, fascinated by the slightly diffuse column of light. Naively, she wondered if someone or something out there in the universe would see her signal. She hoped something would see her shaft of light and know that she existed. That way, she wouldn't feel so alone in the dark. Fascinated by radiance, she wondered how long it would take for the beam to reach a star that she picked out. Now, she could discuss the theories of light endlessly and calculate the travel time but she was much more concerned about what had made the noise in the wood. It could have been an inoffensive animal but she thought not. Animals were not clumsy enough to trip over a root. At the edge of the wood, she flashed her torchlight into the huge dingy palace with myriad brown pillars. The beam bounced between the beeches and a couple of startled squirrels darted up separate trees. No. What she'd heard was bigger than a squirrel. If there was a human being in there, he or she could be hiding behind any of the trunks or could have fled already. "Anybody there?" she cried again.

Nothing.

She walked into the wood, loudly snapping some twigs that had fallen to the floor. Then she turned and played the ray of light on to the other side of the first line of trees. No one. She sighed. It was a hopeless task so she turned back. As soon as she did so, she heard more undergrowth being trampled and crunched underfoot. She spun and, through the mass of trees, the torch just caught a figure – a human figure – beginning to run. Abruptly, Wolfie was at her side and he barked just once. A single terrifying bark to wake the dead. Even Jodie jumped. The fleeing human gasped deeply, like a man, and accelerated as if Satan himself was on his tail.

"Wow!" Jodie shrieked. "I didn't know you had it in you, Wolfie. You fancy yourself as a real guard dog, don't you? Protecting me. Protecting the hand that feeds you."

Without thinking, she patted Wolfie's back. The dog did not sense any threat, so he was content to let her stroke his matted fur for a moment. Finally, they had made friends. But, when Jodie turned, took a few steps back towards the house and said, "Come on. I'll give you a brush," he'd gone. The wood had devoured him. "Oh!" Jodie cried. "You *are* sensitive," she said into the wood. "Don't you like going to the hairdresser's?"

In a different part of the wood, a long sturdy rope dangled like a noose from a bough of a beech tree. Nearby, on the ground, there were seven small wooden boxes with wire mesh doors. Six of the coops were empty. From the other came a frantic fluttering. Higher up, where the pale moonlight gently stroked the canopy of the wood, a figure moved expertly from branch to branch. Not as proficient as a chimpanzee but agile for a human being, he scrambled this way and that, pausing to peer through the foliage and play a torch among the forks in the branches, clearly looking for something. Over his shoulder, he carried a small blanket and a net. Suddenly, he froze as he lay, stretched out along a branch like a snake. Moving his hand slowly and silently, he slipped the net from his shoulder and prepared to drop it on to the bough below. With both hands, he held the net open and then let go so it fell like a parachute. Two seconds later he hissed triumphantly, "Yes!" He scrambled down quickly to collect his trapped prize.

7

Ryan had to admit defeat. He'd beaten Jodie at snooker but, as he expected, he was no competition for her at table tennis. He'd predicted a walk-over at squash, yet she played the game as if her life depended on it. Wherever he put the ball, no matter how wicked or subtle or powerful a shot he managed, she was in the right place. She anticipated every move that he made and she won quite easily. Afterwards, they sat in the café, replacing lost moisture and chatting together. Once his battered pride had healed, he seemed to regard her with even more esteem. "I wanted to ask your advice," he said. "You know about electricity and pylons and all that, don't you?"

Jodie nodded. "Now you're speaking my language."

"I saw a telly programme about it. A documentary. It was saying if you live near a pylon, you can get some type of cancer because of the electric field or something. Is that right? I live almost under that pylon at the other end of the village to you."

"There's no hard evidence," Jodie told him, "but some scientists think there's an association between the electromagnetic fields from power lines and cancers like leukaemia. That's not the same as saying one *causes* the other, though." Jodie paused. "You see, magnetic fields are supposed to be harmless and electric fields flow around, not through, the human body, so it's difficult to make the connection between the fields and problems *inside* the human body. See what I mean?"

"I think so," Ryan responded, trying to keep up with her.

"It's all a bit hazy, though, because a few effects on living systems *have* been confirmed. Not humans, as far as I'm aware, though. Salamanders are knocked unconscious by magnetic fields, that I do know, and homing pigeons get all confused by the changes in magnetic fields when mobile phones are used. So you never know. On top of that, someone's put forward a possible link between electromagnetic fields and cancer. Just recently. It's something about the field attracting the radioactive decay products of natural radon in houses near power lines. But it's all theory. If you're close to a working vacuum cleaner, drill or food mixer you'll experience about the same dose of electromagnetic field as living some metres away from power lines, so I wouldn't worry too much. In Bucks, we're not in a high radon area either. If you tell your parents you want to move, they'll stop doing the vacuuming and cooking in protest."

Ryan smiled at the notion. "You're pretty good at this sort of stuff."

"I can do a bit of research for you, if you like. You'd be amazed what's on the Internet these days."

Ryan shrugged. "OK. If you don't mind. Physics, isn't it?"

"Yes. The study of nature, really. You've got to be in awe of nature – you've got to respect it – to study physics. I inherited the physics gene from my dad."

"And what did you get from your mum? Squash genes?"

Jodie looked away despondently and did not answer.

"Sorry," Ryan murmured. "I didn't mean to… I was only complimenting you on your perform-ance."

"I know," Jodie said. "But, for now, let's keep off the topic of my mum."

Ryan held up his hands in surrender. "Whatever you say."

Jodie took another gulp of ice-cold drink and then said, "You've been in Greenwood End for ages.

It's such a small, quiet place. Don't you ever want to break out?"

Surprised, Ryan answered, "No. I like it. It suits me. Besides," he said, leaning close to her and lowering his voice, "it's impossible to leave. Didn't you know? Once in, you can never escape from Greenwood End." With a sombre expression, he explained in a morbid whisper, "You're in the thick of it. If you tried to get away by going south, you'd come to Medmenham Abbey. Weird place. Scene of mysterious rites and wild orgies of the Hell Fire Club. Sounds modern but it was set up in 1742 by the eccentric Sir Francis Dashwood – just after the death penalty for witchcraft was abolished. The club was active for twenty years. Baboons used to personify Satan in the chapel. All sorts of peculiar goings-on. To the north is the dreaded West Wycombe where Dashwood built a mausoleum. In the dusty corners, there's urns which contain the hearts of the members of his club. The local pub is haunted as well. By Susan. She turned her back on three boyfriends to marry someone posher. After an upperclass husband. The three lads she shunned lured her into the caves in her wedding dress and cracked open her skull. So you wouldn't want to go north or south but you'd fare no better if you tried to escape into Oxfordshire. Stonor Park's haunted. Voices, footsteps and cupboards that open in the house. Outside, its stone circle emits a strange whiff of animals – even though any self-respecting animal won't go near it." Even quieter and more theatrical, he continued, "Only the east left? And no one would dare to venture east from Greenwood End. That way lies … London. Argh!"

Jodie laughed. "Fool!" Really, she was spellbound by the rhythm of his genial voice. She could listen to him all day. "Ghosts!"

"I bet you think it's all done with mirrors," Ryan suggested.

"No," Jodie answered. "I think it's all up here." She tapped the side of her head. "And if it's not all up here, it'll be some natural phenomenon. The interplay of various electromagnetic fields, perhaps."

"Them again!"

"Yes. Maybe they *do* have an effect on humans – including brains." She paused and concluded, "I'll definitely have to check it out."

In the narrow lane near the crossroads in the centre of Greenwood End where The Olde Spotted Dog stood, Ryan's headlights picked out a large obstacle in the road. He braked sharply. When the car skidded to a halt, Jodie and Ryan stared through the windscreen in disbelief. They were looking into the eyes of a stationary pig. "Amazing," Jodie exclaimed. "I thought it was rabbits that froze in headlights. What's a pig doing here anyway?"

Ryan shrugged and got out of the car.

Jodie joined him, standing in front of the inert pig

that took no notice of either them or the chugging car. It was gazing impassively beyond them. It could have been looking into another world. "It seems to be dazed, or something," Ryan murmured.

The shock was wearing off and Jodie was beginning to see the funny side of the pig that continued its impression of a living statue. "Perhaps it's had too much to drink in The Olde Spotted Dog," she ventured with a grin.

Ryan glanced at her askance as if her comment had touched a nerve. But if he knew anything, he decided not to let on. Instead, he picked up on Jodie's good humour. "How could you call the village quiet when you get big stories like this? Imagine the headlines. Pickled Porker Prevents Progress."

Jodie laughed. "In any other place, it'd be 'Pig Runs Amok.' Here, even the drunks just stand around peacefully."

Their sudden joviality seemed to rouse the vacant pig. Her head moved as she took in her surroundings. Clearly, she was bewildered and scared. Scared to be so close to two threatening human beings. On shaky legs, the animal swivelled and tottered away from Jodie and Ryan.

With a puzzled smile on her face, Jodie watched it retreat till it was out of sight.

"Happier now?" Ryan chirped. "It's gone to run amok in the village. Greenwood End joins the big league of news-makers."

Jodie laughed but, getting back into the unobstructed car, she mumbled, "It *was* strange, though."

From the end of the lawn, Jodie called out, "Wolfie! Wolfie. Come and get it." She was glad no one was watching. They would have thought that she was losing her mind. "Wolfie," she repeated in a whisper that she hoped would penetrate the wood.

The dog had been waiting in the safety of the beeches. First he recognized the female's aroma and then her voice confirmed it. He raised his head and sampled the air again. He could not smell any other humans so he walked confidently towards the only one he trusted.

Jodie welcomed him by stroking and patting him. "Yuk," she muttered. "You're a good dog but you do need a clean-up. Come on," she ordered. "Food first." After the meal, Jodie led Wolfie to the back door and invited him in.

From outside, Wolfie sniffed at the air inside the house. One male occupant as well as the woman. He hesitated and looked at Jodie.

"I'll lead the way," she said. "It's perfectly safe. No one's going to hurt you." She beckoned him in from the kitchen.

Still cautious, Wolfie stepped in with his front legs, stretched and sniffed with his black, runny nose. He could not detect any danger so he plucked up courage and padded up to Jodie.

"That's it," she chirped. "Well done. She sat on a chair by the table and Wolfie walked to her, glancing round the room. Jodie put a hand on his rump and pushed slightly, saying, "Sit!" Instead of buckling, his back legs locked defiantly to resist her pressure. "Ah," she murmured. "No one's taught you to sit. Well, why should you anyway? You've got a will of your own."

From the table, the woman produced a hairbrush and immediately Wolfie sniffed it, testing it. He remembered brushes. Occasionally painful but he always felt better after. Not so itchy. This one didn't have Jodie's scent. It belonged to the unknown man.

"It's OK," Jodie told him. "It's Dad's. But you won't catch anything from it," she said with a chuckle, "because I cleaned it first." She set to work on the tangled coat of his flanks. It was a long job but Jodie believed that she was more likely to get Wolfie's cooperation in a brushing than in a bath. She had the feeling that soap and water and a huge, wary dog would not mix. As Wolfie submitted himself to the uncomfortable encounter with the brush, sometimes emitting yelps of protest as Jodie pulled on a particularly matted clump of wiry hair, she whispered reassuringly, "Good boy! You'll be a lot nicer to know afterwards." When she'd finished, she sat back and looked at her handiwork. Not perfect by any means but Wolfie had been transformed.

The scruffy stray had become a majestic hound. She could understand why his breed had once been chosen to hunt wolves and deer. At the shoulder he stood 90 centimetres and she guessed he was slightly heavier than her. About sixty kilogrammes, she thought. Massive but as fast as a greyhound. His face held a pained but proud expression. "What a handsome dog you are! Well done," Jodie congratulated him. "You put up with it well. You look cared for, now." She examined the brush. It was completely snarled with Wolfie's grey hair. And all around the dog there was the fall-out from the operation. Mud, grass, small twigs, probably a good few insects. Jodie groaned. "Another purge required, I think. Dad might notice something's not quite right about his brush if I leave it like this. I'll get you a drink of water," she said, making a fuss of Wolfie, "then I'll clear up the debris." Jodie scrubbed and swept while Wolfie slopped water happily all over the kitchen floor.

Later, she showed him an old blanket that she'd placed in the garden shed. "If you want it," she announced, "it's a bed for you. A bit rough and ready but probably better than what you're used to in the wood. I won't shut the door so you can come and go as you please."

Wolfie sniffed the blanket and tested it with a paw. He recognized what he was being offered by the woman. A long time ago, he'd been trained to sleep in a basket with a similar blanket. At first it was strange but, once he'd impregnated the soft material with his own smell, it had been comfortable and comforting. For some time he hadn't experienced that feeling of luxury and security. Now, he trusted Jodie enough to give it a try. After three unsuccessful attempts to settle, he curled up on the blanket and shut his eyes.

Eleanor sat naked and cross-legged in the room at the end of the corridor with the small urns. She felt nervous, vulnerable and yet full of hope. As the old customs required, at midnight, she had stripped outside by the old well and been sprinkled with its water. The first part of the fertility rites. The freeing of the waters had always signified cleansing, the regeneration of the earth and the origin of new life. Now, she was surrounded by an unbroken circle of hen's eggs, and then, beyond a ring of flickering candles, by her friends and well-wishers who chanted the old songs of fruitfulness. The dark room was filled with their insistent relentless sound. Inside the circle, Eleanor faced a small and bare oak table.

Abruptly, at the Master's signal, the incantation ceased and immediately the coven became vacuous and tense. In anticipation, Eleanor began to shiver. Dressed in a black and crimson cloak, the Master stepped forward carefully, through the rings, carrying a closed basket. With due ceremony, he placed the basket on the table. Standing between Eleanor and the table, he held aloft his hands as if he did not already have silence and attention. Looking into her shadowy face, he intoned, "We, your friends, have come together this night to induce fertility according to the old ways. To dispel barrenness, giving you, Eleanor, an abundant harvest." To put her more at ease, he smiled down at her. From inside the basket there came a plaintive mew but the Master ignored the quiet cry. "Trust in the ancient ritual. From the earliest times, human beings have performed such rites to influence the course of nature. We know that the principle of life and fertility – animal, vegetable or human – is one and indivisible and transferable. Tonight, we call upon a potent magic to allow another creature to pass on to you her powers of reproduction."

The Master of the ceremony took gloves from his pockets and pulled them on. Deliberately, he opened up the wicker basket and drew out a writhing ball of fluff and claws that was Suki the prolific cat. Suki hissed and scratched. The Master whispered treacherous reassuring words to her then, resolutely and expertly, he clamped her at arm's length in one hand while with the other he took the sacrificial knife. Holding Suki above Eleanor, he cried, "From death comes new life."

The gathering gasped and Eleanor winced as she

received Suki's spirit, as one successful mother empowered a mother of the next generation. Eleanor kept her mouth firmly shut. If the slightest crack had appeared, a hideous scream would have escaped. The ritual was horrible but it had to be done. She was desperate for a child and, besides, it was the old way. Wise ways. It would work.

The Master withdrew and the chant began again. The room was filled with the cat's life energy – the exuberant and overpowering sense of creation. In the dimness, the continual incantation became hypnotic and eroded Eleanor's free will and her inhibitions. She abandoned herself to tradition and trance. She absorbed Suki's spirit until she felt drunk and ripe. Soon, she would be reunited with her husband but first there was the dance. The dance around the circle, weaving, unrestrained, trusting the magic of nature that would ensure her wild feet did not crush even a single egg. No longer in command of herself, yet somehow supremely controlled, Eleanor performed the whirling fertility dance impeccably until she was exhausted.

In the sky, nuclear fusion reactions created a spectacular sphere of hot gases large enough to hold over a million planets of the size of the earth in its volume. Five billion years old, the sphere had another five billion years of life before inevitable burn-out, exhaustion and death. For now, the ferocity of the reactions kept the core of the nuclear reactor at 15 million degrees Celsius. In magnetic turmoil, the vast bubbling cauldron produced giant flares and powerful bursts of radiowaves. It also dispensed enough heat and light to sustain life on earth, like a tycoon throwing pennies to the poor. But this brilliant benefactor was also cruel. It also disbursed ultraviolet, X-rays and gamma rays. The atmosphere around the earth had had to learn how to accept the life-giving frequencies and reject the deadly rays before life on the planet surface was possible.

Bright sunshine decorated the Hilliard's kitchen with sparkling warmth. Over breakfast, Jodie chose to confess to her dad that she had acquired a canine companion. "Wolfie. He's in the garden shed," she admitted. "I'm sure he won't be any trouble. And he'll be useful. A good guard dog for the house. You'll let me keep him, won't you?" she implored.

In the morning, her father was not capable of putting up much of a fight. "It's up to you, I guess. You'll have the responsibility. Feeding, walking and so on. If you don't mind all that, a pet could be good for you. A friend."

"Thanks, Dad! I could introduce you to him. I think he'll take to you all right." She said it to try to convince herself as much as her dad.

"I usually handle animals pretty well," he said. "But not now. I'll be back at a sensible time tonight. I'll see him then."

"By the way, Dad," Jodie enquired, "do you know any strong evidence for magnetic fields affecting humans?"

Dr Hilliard stared at his daughter and retorted sharply, "Why do you ask that?"

Taken aback by her father's severe reaction, Jodie replied defensively, "Just that Ryan was interested."

"Ryan?" he snapped suspiciously.

"Yeah. He lives near the power lines and he heard they might be linked to leukaemia."

Her dad's expression softened somewhat. More relaxed, he answered, "Oh, I see. Well, no. There's no strong evidence for power lines causing leukaemia. It's all circumstantial."

"That's what I thought," Jodie added. "Thanks."

Her father lapsed into impenetrable silence.

8

"What exactly is a salamander anyway?" Ryan asked.

"They're … er … a bit like frogs but lizard-shaped," Jodie replied. "Wet, ugly and squidgy. Elongated frogs with poison slime that oozes from their skin. A bit like politicians really."

"Very funny," Ryan muttered. "But you said you had some news for me. I thought you were checking on cancer in human beings near power lines, not squidgy toady things."

"One step at a time," Jodie declared. "I found some old reports on research in America. They start with salamanders and get more interesting. You know, if you cut the tail or a leg off a salamander, it grows another one. It can grow new eye lenses and bits of its heart and brain as well."

"Clever. If only politicians could replace damaged bits of brain…" Ryan put in as he drove towards High Wycombe.

"Apparently, it's an electrical signal that triggers the regeneration," Jodie told him.

"So?"

"Remember, cancer's only out-of-control generation of tissue. Growth gone mad. The salamander regenerates tissue on an electrical cue. Perhaps there *is* a link. The growth of tissue under the influence of electromagnetic signals. Then there's some Eastern Bloc work done in the 1950s. Expose a mouse to a certain electromagnetic pulse and it's dead in three minutes – with no visible physical damage. There's something else as well. I told you strong electrical fields can knock out salamanders. That means there's an effect on their brains. Well, I was wrong about humans. There *are* reports of effects on us. A scientific adviser at the National Radiological Protection Board has found that using a mobile phone can change the temperature of the human brain, would you believe? Some users suffer headaches and ear problems. He wants lower microwave exposure limits." Jodie paused to take a breath and then continued excitedly with the results of her research. "A psychologist discovered that psychiatric patients were admitted to hospitals more when there were solar magnetic storms. Interesting, eh? He reckoned magnetic fields could impair mental performance and induce stress. Perhaps we're not so different from the salamander and mouse after all. Even more intriguing, someone else must have thought there was something in it because, throughout the 1960s, the American Embassy in Russia was bombarded by electromagnetic radiation. Microwaves to be precise."

"Someone trying to cook the ambassadors?" Ryan joked.

"Low level microwaves that wouldn't even pop popcorn," Jodie countered. "No one knew why the embassy was drenched in microwaves. True to form, the Americans didn't tell their own staff. Instead, they brought in a scientist who could study the effects on them in secret. He did. For thirteen years. Higher than average pregnancy abnormalities, two out of four ambassadors died of cancer, there were unusual levels of stress, and one case of rare blood disease. Almost as soon as news of the Moscow Signal, as they called it, leaked out, everything went quiet again. I only traced one more report. It seems the incident persuaded the powers-that-be in the States to explore the biological effects of low frequency electromagnetic radiation. They gave the study a code-name. Pandora. Beyond that, I only found papers that are so heavily censored they're not worth reading. Well…" She paused and then continued, "There was just one more. A reference to an account of a new electronic weapon that came out of the Pandora project. Who knows what that means? I haven't been able to crack it yet. I'd really love to get into a full copy. Find out a bit more about it. Fascinating stuff. Sinister even."

"Yes," Ryan agreed, "but am I going to get leukaemia?"

"The jury's still out on that one," Jodie concluded. "But I don't think we're being told everything. When they clam up like this it usually means there's big money or nasty weapons to be made – or both."

"Another question," Ryan prompted. "Why *are* we going to a pet shop in Wycombe? You don't want to buy some of these salamander things to experiment on, do you?"

"No," Jodie said, cheering up. "We're going for a dog basket, of course. The biggest one they've got."

The wicker basket reeked of almost everything. Rabbits, cats, mustiness, puppies, parrots, mice, bird seed and the whole gamut of pet food. He looked up at his human friend with an expression that said, "Do you expect me to lie in *that*?"

Jodie laughed. She had brought the basket into the kitchen and was trying to persuade Wolfie that it was going to make a comfortable bed. "Straight from the pet shop," she said. "Thought you'd like it. See, I've put your blanket in it." She gave him an encouraging push.

Wolfie stood grumpily in the basket and refused to sit or lie down. As soon as she turned her back, he padded out again.

She spun round and cried, " Oh well. You'll get used to it. I don't suppose it'll feel right till you've broken it in – like a new pair of jeans."

At the sound of a key in the front door, Wolfie barked at the top of his voice. Luckily, the glassware in the kitchen remained intact – but only just. Jodie held on to him by his new collar but she knew that if he decided to make a dash for her dad, she wouldn't be able to stop him. He'd drag her across the floor. "It's OK," she reassured him. "It's only Dad."

Her father stopped outside the door and whispered through the crack, "Is it OK to come in? That was some bark. Is he under control?"

"As much as he'll ever be," Jodie shouted, not daring to issue a guarantee.

Her dad walked nonchalantly into the kitchen, refusing to display trepidation in front of Wolfie. "Mmm," he said. "He's a monster." He smiled, squatted down so that his head was on a level with the dog's and said, "Jodie tells me you're called Wolfie."

Jodie was pleased. Wolfie had not rushed to attack. He was growling, but quietly and without conviction.

"Walk him over to me," her dad suggested.

"OK. Come on," she said to Wolfie. "Come and meet my dad. He's not too bad really."

Wolfie could have refused to budge yet he responded to Jodie's yanking. Besides, he recognized the man's odour. He'd detected it before. It was at its strongest on one of the kitchen chairs and on the brush. And there was another smell near him that Wolfie was keen to explore.

"So far so good," Jodie said, as she reached her dad with Wolfie lagging behind. The dog stayed back but reached forward with a twitching nose.

"I said I was pretty good with animals," her dad remarked. "I use the time-honoured techniques of not being frightened, and bribery." From behind his back he produced an enormous bone in his bandaged hand.

Immediately, Wolfie's eyes lit up and a dripping tongue fell out of his mouth. He walked forward and gingerly accepted the introductory gift.

While Wolfie's teeth were still occupied, Dr Hilliard patted his daughter's companion. The three of them were allies. Together, they decided that Wolfie could sleep in the hall and they placed his new basket in a convenient corner. Every time he let go of his bone, they placed it in the basket. Soon, Wolfie took the hint. He revolved four times round the basket and then plonked himself down with his bone. Even curled up, his back legs overhung the side comically.

Dr Hilliard said to Jodie, "He's all right. Quite nice really." Then he added, "Introduction to companion number one done. One to go, I think."

Jodie frowned but quickly managed a grin. "OK. I'll think about it." She went to her den and continued her quest for information – digging around in dry documents, delving into databases – while she listened to the cellnet calls that her scanner intercepted.

She was interrupted only once by a telephone call from Leah who enthused, "How is he, then? Your new friend."

"Fine," Jodie reported, turning off the scanner. "He's here with me now. I've groomed him, given him a juicy bone, and now he's curled up on a blanket."

There was a slight hesitation before Leah cried, "Ryan? Bone?"

Suppressing a giggle and pretending that she'd misunderstood, Jodie said, "Oh. You meant Ryan! Well, he's fine as well. Not as well groomed, perhaps, but less prone to exercising his teeth on bones. And marginally better at squash."

"Are you trying to tell me you're looking after that dog?"

"He seems to be happy here with me. He slept in the shed last night."

"But you don't know who owns him," Leah objected. "I mean, they could turn up any time and demand to have him back."

"I doubt it," Jodie said. "Whoever it was, they obviously didn't look after him. Probably glad someone else's doing it."

"Anyway," Leah said, "I didn't call about a dog. I want the latest low-down on Ryan."

Jodie answered a hundred questions and confessed, "We're going out tomorrow night. And I'm thinking of inviting him back to the house. Dad wants to vet him, you see."

"You're introducing him to your dad?" she exclaimed. "That's serious!"

"Yeah," Jodie admitted. "Things *are* moving fast. Maybe too fast for me."

Villagers arriving for the midnight meeting in The Olde Spotted Dog glanced up at the sky before entering the pub. The dark segment of the moon was smaller still. There was not much time left.

The followers of the old ways believed that the ancient stone circle harnessed the energy of the sun, the earth and of life itself. The stones trapped the energy and then transmitted it to Greenwood End, ensuring the prosperity and well-being of the village. Before the arrival of the government's Research Station, the scientific community tried to debunk the old lore. They sent a group of scientists to investigate the Greenwood End stone circle and the seventy-seven weather-beaten Rollright Stones set on a high ridge in neighbouring Oxfordshire. For some reason, the investigation was called the Dragon Project. The scientists found the same effect at both sites. At dawn, they detected inexplicable ultrasonic pulses emanating from the standing stones. If anything, the Dragon Project confirmed the theory that the stone circle was a transmitter of energy. Shortly after, the Research Station came and embraced the stone circle within its grounds. The scientists had stolen the village's heritage and tried to prohibit their customs.

The Master of the meeting said, "In four days the moon will be whole again. You know what we must do. Much of the stone circle's energy persists to this day, fuelled by the sun and the earth, but the life energy must be replenished. The old magic has shown us the way. It has singled out a dog – a wolfhound, a hunter, famed for its strength and vital force. For the good of the village, to increase the yields of our farms, the life of this beast must be donated to the stones. Unfortunately, the dog has been adopted by a non-believer. One of the cuckoos. So, each of us has a duty to help to capture the dog, without harming it, if called upon to do so." The Master hesitated, gazing meaningfully at two people in the congregation. "Tonight, we will try to snatch the animal," he announced. "Once we have it, the way is clear. But before the renewal ceremony, we must begin the cleansing rites. We must oust the Research Station – the cuckoos' nest – and reclaim our birthright. The land and the stones. They'll be ours again. Sooner or later, they *will* be ours. Ian has captured what we need to complete the first stage of the cleansing process. As soon as we are assured of having the dog, the cleansing can commence."

Two men trampled through the blackness by torchlight. Compared to the natural inhabitants of the wood, they were ungainly, noisy and sluggish. "This is it," one of them whispered, pointing towards a garden that began at the last line of beeches.

"Sure?" the second queried. "I don't want to knock out some other pet."

"No. This is it, all right."

The first man extracted a joint of meat from his bag and contemplated it for a few moments. "Let's hope it does the trick."

"It won't kill him, will it?"

"No," the man with the meat answered. "He'll eat till he's munched enough drug to knock him out. He can't eat a lethal dose when he's unconscious. That's the idea. I'm hoping it'll last long enough for us to get him back and safely locked up before he comes round again. That's what I'm banking on, anyhow."

"Where do we put it?"

"Our information says he sleeps in the shed so anywhere in the garden will do. The dog'll smell it out. If we leave it in the wood, it's likely something else'll run off with it." He tiptoed into the clearing while his partner kept watch from the shadows. Cautiously, he knelt down, placed the meat behind a stone in the rock garden and then retreated. "Now," he stated, "we make ourselves comfortable. But it won't be long before his nose begins to twitch and he comes out to investigate. Dognapping made easy," he chirped.

One fruitless hour later, the would-be abductors decided to act. "Must be a dozy dog," the first one complained. "I'll go and move the joint right outside the shed and bang on the door to wake him up."

The other man shrugged. He just wanted to get home. "All right. But come back quickly. He could turn nasty."

"The joint'll be more attractive than me."

He stood up, shaking off the cramp in his left foot and hobbled quietly back into the garden. As soon as he knocked on the wooden door of the shed, there was a booming bark. The man hesitated before he ran for it. The low-pitched but loud woof had come instead from the house. He scuttled back to his partner and murmured, "Let's get out of here! The dog's not in the shed at all. He's inside."

The second man clambered to his feet. "What about the meat?"

"Leave it," he decided. "The dog might get it tomorrow. Perhaps someone else'll watch in the morning."

The inept conspirators hurried away.

Woken by Wolfie, Jodie peered out from her curtain. There could have been movement in the wood but she wasn't sure. She crept downstairs and squatted on the hallway carpet. Wolfie walked up to her and she asked, "What's up? Did you hear something?" Together, they went to the kitchen window. Wolfie put his paws on the sill so he could see out as well.

"You did hear something!" Jodie whispered. "Look!"

A fox was prowling near the shed. It stopped over a lump that Jodie took to be a small log of wood. Suddenly, Wolfie detected the fox and began to bark. The fox did not delay. It picked up the log in its mouth and ran for the cover of the beechwood.

"Shhh," Jodie insisted. "Just a fox. Harmless. And you don't want to wake Dad up. He might change his mind about you."

Wolfie obeyed – but only after the fox had disappeared from view. Even then, he left a little warning rumble in his throat.

"Come on," Jodie said, tapping him and walking away from the window. "Bedtime."

9

Under brutal bombardment by high-frequency radiowaves, the water molecules vibrated madly, producing untold heat. The bacon defrosted at speed and in a matter of moments began to cook.

Dr Hilliard had bought one of the more expensive microwave ovens because it guaranteed that radiation leakage was negligible. The user would not be exposed to stray microwaves. He flung open the door and uttered, "You put a lot in!"

"Not really." Jodie defended herself with a smile. "We're cooking for three. One bacon butty for me, two for you and two bits for Wolfie."

Her dad groaned. "OK. You can spoil him for a honeymoon period. A week. But then he gets treated like a normal dog."

After breakfast and her dad's departure, Jodie took Wolfie into the wood for a walk. At night the place seemed eerie and alien but, in the light of day, it was a delightful playground. This time, though, it took Wolfie only five minutes to make it seem creepy again. He found a fox lying flat out on its side. It had been sick and a chunk of meat lay by its side. Jodie cried out in dismay. She thought that it was dead. She bent down to examine the distasteful carcass and Wolfie sniffed at its head. Suddenly, the creature jumped up drunkenly. It was not well. Its brown and white fur was dreary. Its ears sagged woefully its eyes were dull. Bewildered, it attempted to focus on Wolfie's face and then made its escape. As it ran, it staggered and lurched but at least it was recovering. Wolfie charged after the fox and would have caught it easily but Jodie screamed for him to come back. Much to her surprise, he did. She hugged him and murmured, "Good boy."

Wolfie didn't feel hungry so he no longer needed to chase prey. He would have relished the sport of pursuing the fox but not against Jodie's wishes. He dared not make a nuisance of himself. He wanted her friendship and food so he had to behave himself. He had to be faithful. He even tolerated her hugs.

Jodie poked the half-eaten meat with a stick but it seemed perfectly normal. "I don't want you to touch this, Wolfie. It might be bad," she said. She grimaced. "I wonder if it was the fox that came into the garden last night. If it was, it must have been this meat it shot off with. Not a log." She sighed. "So what's a joint of beef doing in our garden and what's wrong with it? Why did it make the fox ill – if it did? Or perhaps," she said, patting Wolfie, "my imagination's working overtime. What do you think?"

Wolfie said nothing but his face was expressive enough. He wanted to get on with the walk. He wanted to investigate more smells, trace the paths of squirrels, mark out his patch.

Back at the house, Wolfie decided to raise the roof again.

"What's up now?" Jodie asked.

But the doorbell answered her question. She had a visitor and Wolfie wanted the world to know. Jodie opened the door just a crack and saw Leah. "Hello," she greeted her friend, shouting above the din of the dog.

Detecting Leah through the gap, Wolfie barked even louder. The poor girl on the doorstep nearly jumped out of her skin. She was clearly frightened.

"Just a minute," Jodie said, shutting the door again. Taking hold of Wolfie's collar and dragging him away, she chastized, "That's not very nice. Leah's a friend. Now you'll have to go in your basket till she's gone." She moved his basket to the kitchen, shut him in, and then returned to her visitor. "Sorry about that," Jodie apologized.

"Don't know what's got into him. He was OK with Dad." Jodie sniffed the air. "Perhaps it's your new perfume."

The colour had drained from Leah's cheeks. "I think it's me," she stammered weakly. "I've never really liked dogs and they always seem to know somehow and bark at me – so I like them even less. I can't win." She shrugged with resignation. "Are you keeping him in the house now?"

"Yes. I tell you, we won't get burgled. No one would dare." Jodie chuckled. "When you come round, I'll put him out if you like. Anyway," Jodie asked, "what brings you here at this time in the morning?"

"Oh, nothing really. I mean … company, I guess. I'm sorry. I didn't know you'd have the dog inside. I ought to be going." Nervously, she eyed the door that led to the kitchen and to Wolfie.

"Don't be silly. You've only just arrived." Jodie didn't appreciate how much Leah had been unsettled by the dog. "I don't want you to be put off just because of Wolfie," Jodie said. "You can still come round. It'll do him good to run around the garden while you're here."

Leah smiled awkwardly. "OK. Maybe next time, then, but I'm off now."

Jodie escorted her to the door, shut it and murmured, "Strange."

She spent the day walking in the wood with Wolfie

or uncovering secrets in her electronics workshop. When she was denied access to the Research Station's computer for the millionth time – or so it seemed – she went in search of Pandora again. By the time that Ryan called for her, she was impatient to show him what she had discovered.

Wolfie emitted his lukewarm growl at Ryan but there was no serious intent behind it. At the door, Ryan said, "So this is Wolfie the dog." He put out his hand confidently and Wolfie sniffed at it tentatively. "Is he coming with us tonight?"

Jodie stood to one side. "I thought you might like to…" She nodded towards the inside of the house. "Stay here."

"Really?"

"You said you wanted to see my gadgets, as you called them."

"All right," Ryan responded, stepping inside. He glanced into Jodie's face and guessed, "That's not all. What else am I going to see?"

"Information."

"And?"

"Wolfie."

"And?"

Jodie laughed tentatively. "OK. I confess. Dad. He wants to get a look at you. He's not back yet but you can wait."

Ryan groaned. "The mad professor. Do I have to?"

Jodie nodded. "I think so. You better come in and take a seat. We've got some talking to do first. You need to be briefed."

Ryan could tell by her expression that she was solemn so he didn't indulge in any more banter. "All right," he agreed, equally sober.

Once they sat in the lounge, Wolfie stretched out on his side between them. He used up a considerable proportion of the floor space. Jodie looked up from the carpet and muttered, "If you're going to see Dad, you'd better know a bit more about us. For better or for worse." She exhaled slowly and then breathed in as much courage as she could muster. "It's not just that he struggles to come to terms with the locals' opinion of him. Not just that he's suspicious about locals like you. There's something else and it's nothing to do with you or Greenwood End or his work. You see, before we were here, we lived in London. Dad, me and Mum. One day, a year and a half back, Mum decided to go into town on the bus. Like millions of people do every day. The trouble is, some terrorist went on the same bus..." She looked at Ryan who was staring at her, anticipating the horror that she was about to reveal. His face betrayed wariness and disapproval. "He – or she – they couldn't tell afterwards – was carrying a ... device, as they euphemistically called it, into the City. He didn't get there. The bomb went off early." Jodie leaned back in her chair and sniffed. For a few seconds she gritted her teeth and clung to her emotions by her fingertips. "The ... er ... bus was reduced to a tangle of metal. For months, all I could see when I shut my eyes was the skeleton of that bus. Bent outwards. Who knows what Dad saw when he closed his eyes? He didn't sleep for ages – unless he took what the doctor prescribed." She sighed and held herself together. "So you see, he has his problems. He can't forget. He can't forgive. It's screwed him up. He'll be OK with you, I think, but sometimes he can't get out of his head the idea that anyone who gets close to me is wanting to ... harm me as well."

Ryan was shaking his head poignantly. "I'm sorry, Jodie. I didn't know." He was kicking himself for his quip about her mum's squash genes. It must have hurt her. And he had another reason to feel uneasy but he couldn't bring himself to confess it.

Jodie stood up, cursed under her breath and turned her back on him. "Silly me," she muttered. She wiped her eyes and, without turning, said, "I'll ... er ... go and get us a coffee." Sympathetically, Wolfie woke up and padded after her into the kitchen.

It wasn't going to be a fun evening after all. Ryan squirmed and stayed in his seat. He guessed it was one of those times when trying to console her could result in making matters worse. One careless, amateurish word could do it. Besides, confronted with such an awful tragedy, what could he say?

When Jodie returned, she had two mugs of coffee, her composure and a less difficult topic of conversation. "Come on," she said. "While we wait for the man who matters, I'll show you something. My cubby-hole. You said you wanted to see all the gadgets. And I want you to see a report."

It was a mess really. Jodie was the first to admit it. But it was an engaging mess. An orderly workshop would be a sign of apathy or insanity. No one would accuse Jodie of indifference. She had assembled a disorderly Aladdin's cave of electronic equipment. A chaotic cobweb of wires dangled and stretched from one end of the room to the other. The computer seemed to be hooked to everything in sight. A telephone and a fax. Discs, CD-ROMs and manuals littered the work-top. A tuner, amplifier and scanner were stacked haphazardly. In two corners of the room, speakers were balanced on shelves and appeared to be on the verge of instability. On the screen of the monitor, two coloured loops writhed playfully like hyperactive worms mating. At one moment they were knotted together and then they slipped over each other, freeing themselves, and resumed the pursuit.

In the doorway of the lair that had once been a spare bedroom, Ryan hesitated. "I hardly dare come in at all," he said. "I'll knock something over and break it."

Jodie put down the coffees and smiled at him. In

a schoolteacher's voice, she said, "Come in. Sit down, behave and don't fidget."

Automatically and eerily, the voice-activated cassette recorder turned itself on when the quiet crackles from the speakers were displaced by a ghostly male voice saying, "Yes, it's me. I need the … goods. Tomorrow night. A professional job this time. Direct injection."

Jodie explained, "The scanner's picked up a mobile phone conversation – or one half of it. Sounds juicy."

The same voice from the same unseen man continued, "It's not critical, is it? I don't know exactly, but it's big."

Unable to resist the opportunity, Jodie set to work with her sniffer, trying to lock on to the other half of the call. Ryan listened to the scheming voice with a puzzled expression. The man could have been standing in the room with them, whispering his message, but he was nowhere to be seen. Ryan shivered. It reminded him of purported encounters at the foot of the haunted cellar stairs in Hughenden Manor. A disembodied voice. Uncanny.

"Yes. It must be about that. Anyway, you know what's needed. No risks. No accidents. When you work out the dose, just don't make any mistakes. It's for a short trip. No overdose, no death."

Jodie glanced at Ryan with raised eyebrows. "Another drug deal," she surmised in a whisper.

Her efforts to locate the other end of the brief exchange failed. The frequency cleared as the telephone call ended. "Missed," she grumbled. "Oh, well. That's not really why we're here." She turned off the cassette and then dismissed the screen saver with a jolt of the mouse. "This is what I wanted you to see. It took ages but I got into a small section of a Pandora report. Here it is. I downloaded it on to my hard disk." She picked up her coffee and took a sip. "Have a read," she invited him, "and tell me what you make of it."

A short introductory paragraph identified the excerpt as a part of a US Air Force Review of Biotechnology in 1982, concerning a new electronic weapon developed during the Pandora investigation. The weapon was said to involve magnetic energy resulting from radiofrequency radiation which it abbreviated to RFR.

RFR fields may pose powerful and revolutionary anti-personnel military threats. RFR experiments and the increasing understanding of the brain as an electrically mediated organ suggests the serious probability that impressed electromagnetic fields can be disruptive to purposeful behaviour. Further, the passage of approximately 100 milliamperes through the myocardium can lead to cardiac standstill and death, again pointing to a speed-of-light weapons effect. A rapidly scanning RFR system could provide an effective stun or kill capability over a large area.

"You're out to shock tonight, aren't you?" Ryan observed softly. "I don't know what this means precisely," he said, "but it sure ain't good news."

"It means there's a new weapon under development. One you can't see, smell, hear or feel. And it stuns or kills."

Ryan shuddered again. "That's an appalling thought," he murmured.

Jodie nodded. "Using electromagnetic radiation for war, it's disgusting."

They looked into each other's faces. Huddled like a couple of spies in front of the computer screen, Ryan was so close to her, it seemed entirely natural to lean forward slightly and kiss her. Lightly, briefly. The fleeting contact signified affection and provided comfort at a time of apprehension and outrage. In the kiss there was also condolence for the wrong committed against Jodie's mum. There was a recognition of sorrow. There was mutual acceptance of the inevitable. A meagre touch of the lips, a simple act, but it expressed so much.

Ryan pulled away and, not referring to the kiss at all, whispered, "You know, I looked up Pandora as well. The first woman on earth, she was. Created by Zeus to plague all men. He gave her beauty and charm but he sprinkled in a great deal of curiosity. Remind you of anyone at all?" He reached out and touched her shoulder but did not wait for a reply. He continued, "To punish all men, Zeus gave Pandora a box and told her never to open it. You see, it contained all the diseases, disasters and troubles of the world and they would've stayed locked away but Pandora opened the box. Zeus knew she would, because of that incredible curiosity. She released all those horrible things on us – just as Zeus wanted." Ryan sighed. "I really like you, Jodie, but I'm worried about all this stuff you're finding out. It's dangerous and I don't want you to get hurt. *Your* Pandora's box is this computer. It might be best left unopened."

Jodie was touched by his concern but she replied, "It's information, Ryan. That's all. It can't hurt us."

Ryan paused, thinking. Then he asked, "Do you know what was left in Pandora's box when she slammed the lid back on? Just one item."

Jodie shook her head.

"Hope," Ryan said bluntly.

Wolfie leapt up and barked. The front door was opening. For a moment, Jodie and Ryan didn't move. They looked vacantly at each other. Then Jodie broke the spell. "Saved by the bell," she quipped, trying to renew their spirits. In Ryan's ear, she breathed, "Your next ordeal awaits." She led him downstairs by the hand.

10

By the time that Jodie and Ryan stood in front of her dad, their hands had uncoupled and Dr Hilliard was patting Wolfie in welcome. "Ah," he said, artificially cheerful. "You must be Ryan." He shook the young man's hand and then smiled at Jodie. Pointedly, he glanced at their mugs of coffee and asked, "Any left for me?"

She nodded. "I'll go and pour." Wolfie trudged after her.

Left alone with Dr Hilliard, Ryan shuffled restlessly. "Jodie was showing me her electronic stuff. Impressive."

"Let's take a seat," Jodie's dad said, walking into the living room. "You can call me Michael," he declared. "Mr Hilliard would be all right but it's wrong and Dr Hilliard sounds far too formal."

"OK," Ryan agreed. He tried to strike up a conversation. He was used to chatting to strangers. He'd got the job at the old house because he was supposed to be a natural at talking – a spontaneous and amiable communicator. He certainly wasn't a bumbling idiot so he tried not to act like one. But it was the girlfriend's dad and Jodie had unnerved him. "Jodie told me you work up at the Research Station," he said lamely, as if he didn't already know, as if he didn't know about the mad professor tag.

"That's right." The physicist didn't expand. Instead he asked, "And what about you? Still at school, college or what?"

When Jodie returned with her faithful hound in tow and a drink for her dad, Ryan was explaining his work at Hughenden Manor. They indulged in small talk until Jodie interjected, "Dad, I … er … told Ryan about Mum."

Her father frowned but said, "Well, I suppose these things are best out in the open."

"I think so," Jodie replied, nodding.

With a curiously uninterpretable expression, Michael asked Ryan, "And how did you react to the news?"

Ryan hesitated. He knew that he was being tested. He knew that tact was required. He also knew that Jodie would rescue him if he delayed any more. In a way, he didn't want to be rescued. He wanted to make a brave, sensible and sensitive contribution. "I think… I think some people, like the terrorist on the bus, are blinded by their own aims," he said. "They're so blinkered by what they believe in, they choose to ignore the consequences. They don't see the suffering they cause."

Jodie issued a sigh of relief, flashed a fragile smile at him, and even felt faintly proud of his mini-speech.

Her dad spoke in a quiet but dangerously distant and disturbed voice, "I think you'll find terrorist groups attract psychopaths like excrement attracts flies. And you didn't say they have to be stopped before they do any more damage."

Quite reasonably, Ryan queried, "Is that possible?"

Without a trace of hesitation or doubt, Michael Hilliard replied, "We could eliminate quite a lot of it. We *will*." He didn't elaborate.

To change the subject, Jodie turned to her dad and enquired unwisely, "Have you heard of the Pandora project, Dad?"

For an instant, he looked shaken but then he recovered and mumbled, "Yes … I vaguely remember something. Why?"

"I came across a report on it. I wanted you to tell me what you knew."

Abruptly, her dad became sullen. "It's not the sort of thing you need to get involved in," he snarled. Then he walked out of the room, leaving behind half of his coffee.

Wide-eyed, Ryan gazed at Jodie questioningly.

She shrugged. "I don't know what I said," she whispered, "but I warned you nothing was easy with Dad."

"Hardly surprising under the circumstances," Ryan put in. "But at least he agrees with me. It's not the sort of thing you should be getting involved in."

Jodie chose not to respond to his caution.

Shortly after, Jodie and Ryan went out on their own. Actually, not quite on their own. They were chaperoned by Wolfie. And, unbeknown to them, they were followed by two men in a blue estate car.

Jodie did not really feel like enjoying herself so she got Ryan to drive her home early. Outside her house, she pecked him on the lips and murmured, "Sorry I'm not good company tonight."

Ryan smiled wryly. "I understand," he replied.

She wished him goodnight and went inside.

Almost immediately, Jodie's dad announced, "Before I forget, Leah called. Said she'll come round tomorrow night – as long as you put Wolfie outside. Does that make sense?"

"Yes," Jodie replied. "Thanks."

"What's it all about? Doesn't she mix with Wolfie?"

Hearing his name for the second time, Wolfie

strolled up to Dr Hilliard to receive a pat on the head.

"She doesn't mix with any dog, as far as I know," Jodie answered. She plonked herself down and then looked at her father. "Dad," she began. "It's been a while since you talked to me about physics. You used to make it so thrilling. The great discoveries. Black holes, spinning neutron stars and the Big Bang. The mind-bogglingness of nature. When other kids got fairy tales, I got exciting physics. You don't do that much now."

"No. I regret it." He sighed and took another gulp of whisky. "I guess I'm busier now. And you know I don't talk – *can't* talk – about the job."

"You're not busy right now. No Ryan. And Wolfie can keep a secret. Will you tell me about the Pandora project?"

Pouring himself another drink, her father said, "I'm worried about you. You and this Ryan. Since he's been around, you've been asking some funny questions about electromagnetic radiation, humans and Pandora." He took his drink and, Jodie noted with alarm, the whole bottle back to his seat. Wolfie twitched his nose and moved further away from the alcohol. "Are you sure he's not using you to get information about the Research Station's work from me?"

Jodie was about to say something rash but thought better of it.

"Aplin," her dad continued. "I think I *have* heard that name mentioned at work. When I've got the time, I'd better get Security to look into it."

She could not bite her lip any more. "Ryan's all right!" Jodie cried. "It's me that's nosy about Pandora. You know what I'm like."

"So does he. He got you started with the power lines business, knowing it would lead to me and Pandora."

"Dad," Jodie uttered plaintively. "You've had a bad time, I know, but you can't see enemy spies everywhere you look. You're imagining it. It's not there."

Her father sighed. "I guess you're right – as usual. But I think I'm right to be wary. A security check can't do any harm if he's as clean as you say."

Reluctantly, knowing that she couldn't prevent it if her dad was determined, Jodie muttered, "I suppose it'll help if it puts your mind at rest."

"Now," he said, pouring himself another whisky, "Pandora. This stays between you and me, Jodie. Right?" Revealing more than he would have done if he hadn't been drinking, he lowered his voice and remarked, "You've found out anyway, as far as I can gather. The Pandora team in the States discovered that a strong RFR pulse *does* have an effect on the brain. Rats, sheep, humans. It doesn't matter. Certain radiofrequencies disorientate brains. It's staggering," he said, smiling a little insanely at his unintentional pun. "We don't know precisely how or why but it means we have to think again about how our bodies and brains work. You see, cells are supposed to block penetration by low-frequency electromagnetic radiation. And indeed they do. They filter out almost all of it like the atmosphere filters out hazardous radiation from the sun. But there's a tiny band of radiofrequencies that seems to find a window. Whoosh! Straight through. They're probably the same frequencies that cells use to communicate naturally with each other. It's just a matter of tuning in to that window and an RFR pulse finds a way in. We've found that what exactly you shine in determines what biological effect you get. Some radiation seems to *improve* abilities, some distorts perceptions and causes stress. Some causes instantaneous knock-down."

"So, you *are* working on it," Jodie mumbled. "Why haven't we heard about this before?" she asked.

"Because the population is constantly exposed to electromagnetic radiation. Power lines, telecommunications, radar and so on. The Government wants to play down the link between RFR fields and health or everyone will panic."

"And because they'd object to weapons development?"

"Would they? I'm not so sure. People accept that the authorities use guns. An electronic device is far more humane and sophisticated. It's a superb stun weapon, Jodie. It has the potential for counteracting terrorism," he said animatedly, revealing his true motives. "I shouldn't be telling you this, but imagine a kidnap or hijack, for example. One helicopter overhead, a pulse of RFR and terrorists will be knocked out immediately for hours. Victims will be knocked unconscious as well, of course, but they recover. No problem. Think of the advantages for peacekeeping, crowd control, riots, almost any breach of security in prisons, military establishments and the like."

"And what about killing? Can an RFR pulse cause death?" Jodie enquired bleakly.

"Death?" her father repeated. A little drunk, he replied, "I guess it's not impossible, but it's not on our agenda as far as I know."

Jodie thought sadly that even if the Research Station did want to develop its weapon to the ultimate end, her dad might turn a blind eye to it. In his head, a battle would be raging. He knew killing was wrong but the vengeful part of him would want to blow away each and every terrorist. He might not take the extra step himself but perhaps he would tacitly agree to others providing a means of retribution.

While Jodie and her father were closeted inside, exchanging secrets like informants, the stones were huddled together on the lonely heathland. Their circle looked like a clandestine meeting of scheming ancients.

The new generator was connected to the probe which was clamped above a transparent plastic case. The probe dangled down like an ominous, blood-thirsty sword. Below it, unaware of the danger, five white hamsters cringed. They should have been scrambling over each other, playing, eating. But these hamsters were held in a bare cage, clamped to the spot. Their heads and parts of their bodies had been shaved down to wrinkly grey skin. Electrodes were attached to the ugly patches and some had been bored through the skull into specific parts of the brain. The electrodes stood out from their heads like cruel aerials.

Carefully, the Director of the laboratory checked the connections. Standing between the three technicians and the cage, he held up his hands and, with due ceremony, pronounced that the experiment could proceed. "We'll use the settings that Michael Hilliard developed but increase the amplitude ten times." From inside the case there came a plaintive squeak but the Director ignored the quiet cry. "We've performed lots of experiments to stun. As a result, we know the precise parameters for a knock-down weapon. Any fatalities have just been mistakes. Miscalculations of power on the way to perfecting an effective stun. Tonight, we're going to push our understanding – and our aims – a little further. The probe will deliver the most potent pulse of RFR ever generated in a controlled laboratory experiment."

The Director leaned over the plastic cage and whispered treacherous reassuring words to the hamsters and then, with his technicians, he withdrew to the adjoining room that was screened from the directional RFR pulse. Three of the researchers gathered round the television like a coven of witches round a cauldron and watched the video close-up of the hamster cage. The last technician stood by the control panel and waited for the Director's word. Kate Lawrence was wondering why they had been told to conduct the experiment late, after Dr Hilliard's departure. She assumed it was because he might not have approved. She was feeling uneasy about the whole thing. Dispassionately, the Director said, "All ready. Everything's up and running, computers on and monitoring functions of all subjects. Let's go."

Reluctantly, but having no choice, Kate flicked the switch.

Instantly, manic traces of overwhelmed brain and body functions were transmitted to the hungry computers. In the cage all five creatures were incapacitated immediately. Stupefied and transfixed like waxworks. Their wild eyes bulged with surprise and shock. Crushing stress burst apart the hearts of three of the hamsters within four seconds. Less fortunate, the other two endured another second or two of tortured life before their brain stems succumbed to the invisible and deadly radiation. Coherent nerve transmissions reduced to meaningless confusion. Grey matter obliterated.

In disgust, Kate averted her eyes from the television screen.

Even before the results were examined in detail, it was obvious from the swift despatching of the animals that the experiment had been totally successful.

"Very satisfactory!" the Director pronounced, putting his hands behind his head and sitting back. "I'll leave you to clear up. In the morning I'll begin to analyse the data. Thank you all. A job well done."

From death would come new knowledge.

Jodie was scared that her dad was in deeper water than he cared to admit. If an RFR pulse could kill, as the US report had claimed, the weapon was no longer merely a convenient peace-keeping device. Whole battlefields of soldiers could be wiped out in a few moments by a low-flying aircraft that could blanket the area with electromagnetic energy. Maybe it could kill everyone in a city. Any person, group or nation at odds with the owners of such an RFR weapon would not be safe. It was a truly horrifying prospect. Maybe her dad's predecessors hadn't realized the full horror at first. Maybe, by the time they cottoned on, it was too late. To quash any opposition to the development, to eradicate resistance, maybe the authorities had had to remove the previous two scientists in devious ways. It was possible that their deaths had nothing to do with ruthless villagers or suicide, after all.

Jodie wanted to know more. She did not share Ryan's worries about information. Quite the opposite. She was worried about a lack of information. The next morning, she found a computer address for the Research Station secreted within its Web site. Then she used Telnet, a program allowing her to log on to a computer at a remote site, to bang metaphorically on the door of the Research Station. The occupants seemed disinclined to answer, though. At the log-on prompt, she typed in *Pandora* as a password and the system responded by denying her access. She suffered a similar rebuttal when she tried *Pandora_Project*. Authorization failure. The same fate awaited *Project_Pandora* and *Pandora_ RFR*. Jodie sat back and groaned. "You can lead a hacker to an address," she muttered to herself, "but you can't make her enter." She'd thought of the variants on *Pandora* as a password to the Research Station's computer last night, when her dad had admitted to the existence of the project and painted such a glossy image of it. It seemed, though, that her bright idea was flawed. One more rejected password and the system would shut her out as an unwanted intruder. Suddenly and ironically inspired by something that Ryan had said to her when he'd doubted the wisdom of wanting to learn more, she entered *Pandora's_Box*. Abruptly and unexpectedly, the Research Station's system welcomed her with open arms. She had been logged on as a legitimate user.

Absorbed in hacking, Jodie didn't notice that, behind her Wolfie was taking great joy in mangling one of her dad's slippers.

On the screen, she was presented with a number of folders to explore and she double-clicked on the one labelled *RFR*. The door opened on a bewildering number of reports and technical detail. "Where do I start?" Jodie asked herself. Randomly, she clicked on one document that revealed a lot of boring information about budgets and personnel. The next file contained the findings of innocuous experiments with different generators of radio-frequency pulses. She was locked out of tantalizing files called *rfrlamb.doc* and *rfrhuman.doc*. They were protected by further passwords. She was unable to leapfrog from unclassified data banks into higher security files. They were probably encoded and monitored. She cursed and gave up. But she learned that the Research Station had information that had to be severely restricted, even if she didn't know what it was. She feared the worst.

Instead, she left Wolfie with the other slipper to chew and went into High Wycombe on the bus to buy her dad a new pair of slippers and to visit the library. In the reference section, Jodie scanned through records of the local newspapers. Evidently, the first scientist to become an apparent victim of suicide died four years ago. A Dr Kennard. The coroner's conclusion was controversial but the tone of the article suggested agreement. The reporter had dug up Kennard's past and found an unstable, sorry character, riddled with depression. The article had nothing to say about when the depression had started – and what had caused it. Jodie searched out the second suicide. Either the newspaper had struggled to discover anything at all about the next victim, Professor Anthea Nevin, or maybe the reporter had lost interest. A few short paragraphs, published almost exactly a year ago, stated that Professor Nevin had been ill for a while with the symptoms of stress. She was reported to have suffered headaches, nausea, fatigue, confusion and paranoia. All acute symptoms of stress. Talking to herself, Jodie murmured significantly, "All symptoms of RFR exposure as well, I bet." The newspaper article went on to explain that the professor had walked calmly into the woods nearby, sat down against a tree and swallowed a chemical cocktail of poisons that she must have prepared in the laboratory beforehand. A rambler had stumbled across her body four days after her disappearance.

A month later, Jodie contemplated, Dr Hilliard stepped into Anthea Nevin's shoes. Jodie sighed and turned off the reader. She didn't believe a word of the stories. She assumed that, in conducting RFR experiments, the two physicists had been exposed to a lethal dose by accident or by design and the authorities had covered it up. She left the library even more worried about her dad. Since the death of her mum, he'd been near the edge or even tottering on it. He'd moved out of London and taken the post at the Research Station to start afresh. Now it seemed to Jodie that his job was more likely to provide the final push.

Jodie went home and set her modem and computer to intercept any fax messages going into the Research Station.

That evening, the blue estate car was parked discreetly near the Hilliard's house while, inside, Jodie was entertaining Ryan in the lounge. Her father had not returned from work when the phone rang and Leah proclaimed that she was about to set out. Jodie smiled and, after she'd put down the phone, said to Ryan, "I think I've just been give my instructions. Leah'll arrive in a few minutes. I'd better put Wolfie out."

Dragged by his collar, the disgruntled dog submitted unwillingly to her yanking. "Get some fresh air for a bit," she said. "You'll love it." To soften the blow, she also allowed him to take a bone and one of the tattered slippers with him. As soon as Leah arrived, Wolfie protested loudly at being excluded, but he calmed down after a while and returned to gnawing the smelly slipper. Only Wolfie could fathom its attractions.

Leah seemed more jittery than normal. Jodie put it down to Ryan's unexpected presence. Leah was torn between her friendship with Jodie and curiosity over their relationship – and maybe jealousy. One of her unspoken questions was answered silently when Ryan put his arm round Jodie's shoulders and she didn't shrug him off. In fact, she nestled against him. In a quiet unassuming way, Ryan and Jodie seemed proud to announce their status. And it was an announcement. Once Leah knew something, the rest of Greenwood End would know it by the next day.

The three of them talked, had a few drinks and listened to a few CDs until Leah could no longer ignore the uncomfortable role of gooseberry. She got up to leave just as Dr Hilliard arrived. Their paths crossed in the hallway.

Jodie's dad observed, "It's like Euston Station in here, but…" He frowned.

"What?"

"Where's Wolfie?"

"Outside in the garden," answered Jodie.

"Then why hasn't he barked?" her dad asked.

Jodie dashed to the back door, opened it and called, "Wolfie! Wolfie!"

There was no answer. The dog had gone.

11

The narrow shafts of white light penetrated the wood, probing each clearing, each trunk. It was, of course, a hopeless task. Scanning with one torch, Jodie called, "Wolfie! Here, boy!" A few paces away, Ryan's beam was not as effective but he cast it about for signs of Jodie's dog anyway. Really, he was in the wood to support Jodie more than to find her wolfhound. The dog's sudden departure had distressed Jodie and Ryan felt sorry for her. "I *can't* believe he's gone back to the wild," she uttered. "Even if he didn't want to be put out tonight, he wouldn't run away. He was happy with me!"

"Perhaps he just chased something into the wood and got carried away?" Ryan suggested. "Didn't realize how far he'd gone."

"Then he'd be back by now. He knows his way round the wood and he'd come to my voice. The other day, he stopped chasing a fox when I called him." Her voice betrayed growing desperation.

"Well," Ryan said, "I don't think we're doing any good out here. I'm sorry but I think we might as well go back – before *we* get lost." He shone his torch on to his watch and added, "Besides, I promised my mum I'd be back a while ago to help her out with a job."

Jodie sighed. "You're right, I know, but let's give it another minute." She peered along the ray of light again and bellowed into the void, "Wolfie!"

It was useless. After five more minutes, they headed back to the house. Jodie prepared a big bowlful of dog food and left it by the dustbin. Then she bid goodnight to Ryan and thanked him for his help.

"I've got a couple of days off, starting tomorrow," Ryan told her. "Do you want me to come round in the morning?"

Jodie jumped at the chance. "Yes," she replied sorrowfully. "In the circumstances, I could use the company."

Optimistically, Ryan said, "You might need someone like me to celebrate his homecoming with." He took her by the shoulders and kissed her gently.

Jodie responded half-heartedly.

The first stage had begun. In a black and crimson cloak, the Master chanted the ancient words that in olden days were roared at unwelcome outsiders, whispered over victims of the plague, wailed in the presence of those possessed by the devil. The spell had been used to purge the village and the people of bad influences, disease and evil spirits. Now, with six followers, the Master stood outside the fence of the despised Research Station and demanded another purging. In the middle of the night, only his face shone ghostlike in the dim light. After the words came the deeds. On his unspoken signal, a nod of his detached head, the villagers squatted down by the coops at their feet. The Master took the lead. His cruel, grasping hand reached into the box where a tiny heartbeat would soon be extinguished in the name of the cleansing. His six companions followed suit.

Jodie didn't sleep. She dozed by her bedroom window so that she could survey that moonlit wood. Nearly a full moon. But no Wolfie. In the morning, the bowl of food remained depressingly uneaten.

As soon as Ryan arrived, Jodie asked him to accompany her to the village shop. "I've got an idea," she muttered. In the store, she selected two token items and took them to Marissa. Before the storekeeper could ask after her father, Jodie enquired, "Has anyone been in for dog food?"

Marissa was taken aback by the unusual question, "Er… yes."

"Who?" Jodie queried.

At the till, Marissa shrugged. "People with dogs," she said blankly and uncooperatively.

"I mean," Jodie explained, "has anyone started buying dog food for the first time?"

Marissa shook her head. "I can't say they have."

Disappointed, Jodie murmured, "OK. Thanks."

"Is your dad still at…?" Marissa began.

Jodie interrupted her impatiently. "Yes. And he's still alive." She grabbed Ryan's hand and walked out of the shop.

Back at Jodie's house, Ryan requested a second hearing of the telephone conversation that she had pirated on the day before yesterday.

"The drugs deal?"

"Yes," Ryan confirmed. "You recorded it, didn't you?"

"Yes. Why?"

"Because… Well, let me hear it again and I'll tell you after."

Jodie shrugged. "OK." On the way upstairs, she remarked glumly, "You know, Wolfie's only been around for a few days but the place seems so empty and quiet without him."

In her retreat, Ryan gave her a brief hug and said, "Play me the tape. Let's see if that helps at all."

Downcast, Jodie retorted, "I don't know how it could." But she replayed the cassette, anyway.

Yes, it's me. I need the ... goods. Tomorrow night. A professional job this time. Direct injection.

4 seconds gap.

It's not critical, is it? I don't know exactly, but it's big.

3 seconds gap.

Yes. It must be about that. Anyway, you know what's needed. No risks. No accidents. When you work out the dose, just don't make any mistakes. It's for a short trip. No overdose, no death.

When it had finished, Ryan said, "You know, it *could* be a drugs deal. But not the sort you're thinking of."

"What do you mean?"

"Well, what if you recorded someone who wanted to kidnap a dog the next day? That would be yesterday. He wants something to make the job easier."

On the same wavelength as her boyfriend and suddenly animated, Jodie interjected, "You mean, he's talking about injecting a dog with a tranquillizer?"

Ryan nodded. "It's possible. No more than that, but it *is* possible. Sounds to me as if he was ordering a knock-out drug. When he said, 'Goods,' he meant something that would make Wolfie unconscious for a bit. Then he could take him away – on a short trip."

It could be he wasn't talking about a *drugs* trip at all."

"Yes! You're not as daft as you look, are you?" Jodie said, realizing that there was hope for finding Wolfie after all. Stagnation grieved her intensely but as long as she could see a way forward, Jodie remained hopeful. She squeezed Ryan's arm and went into overdrive. "The supplier – the one we couldn't hear – was asking how heavy Wolfie was, I bet. He'd need to know that to work out the right drug dose. A little dog would need a little dose and a big dog like Wolfie would need more. It all makes sense!" She hesitated and then said, "I need to play it again and try to guess the response. Like a jigsaw. See what fits the gaps." She rewound the tape and played it again, acting the part of the unheard caller, guessing the missing words. On the fourth attempt, she hit upon responses that completed a sensible conversation.

"Yes, it's me. I need the ... goods. Tomorrow night. A professional job this time. Direct injection."

In the interval, Jodie inserted, "OK. What dosage? How heavy is the dog?"

"It's not critical, is it? I don't know exactly, but it's big."

Jodie slipped in the next question. "Is it, say, sixty kilograms?"

"Yes. It must be about that. Anyway, you know

what's needed. No risks. No accidents. When you work out the dose, just don't make any mistakes. It's for a short trip. No overdose, no death."

Jodie turned off the cassette and cried, "It fits beautifully. I bet it was something like that." Then she moaned, "Someone drugged Wolfie and took him away." Suddenly thoughtful, Jodie continued, "You know, this makes sense of something else. I'm pretty sure, the night before I recorded this message, someone left poisoned meat in the garden for Wolfie. A fox got in instead but I bet it was meant for Wolfie. Attempt number one. Failed. That's why the chap on the tape said he wanted a professional job this time. Last night was attempt number two to drug him. The successful one," she fretted.

"Yes," Ryan agreed. He glanced at Jodie, adding, "And don't you think our mystery person must be the local vet – or a chemist?"

Jodie nodded slowly. "You might be right. Someone who knows about tranquillizers. Vet or pharmacist, to be precise."

Full of revelations, Ryan said, "What's more, I'm pretty sure whose voice we heard. I think it's Ben Godwin from The Olde Spotted Dog," he reported. "I thought it was when I first heard it but I wasn't sure. Now, listening again, I'm as near certain as I can be."

"Ben Godwin." Jodie grunted his name as if it were a dirty word.

"One more thing," Ryan muttered, not daring to look into Jodie's face as he delivered bad news. "Remember what I said about the Hell Fire Club? Dashwood, 1742 and all that? Well, there's something else I ought to tell you about Greenwood End. It's not as sleepy as you think. You see, there's a modern version of the Hell Fire Club in the village. An outsider like you wouldn't qualify for membership. But it meets in The Olde Spotted Dog."

Jodie had a hundred questions but first she enquired, "What's this got to do with Wolfie?"

"There's worse to come," Ryan admitted. "I'm getting to it. In my year at school, there was a kid called Ian Rickley. I didn't mix with him much. I remember only two things about him. He was always climbing things. He could climb anything, anywhere. And he once said there's a place in the pub where they've got these small pots. Urns. I didn't pay it any attention at the time but..." He breathed in noisily and then carried on, "Sorry, Jodie, but Dashwood was reputed to keep a heart of a sacrificial victim in each of his urns."

"What?" Jodie exploded. Aghast, she cried, "Your not trying to tell me..."

"Sorry," he repeated. "I thought it was Ian's sick sense of humour or overactive imagination but ... maybe not."

"You think they're going to ... sacrifice Wolfie and put his heart in..." Jodie covered her face.

"That's horrible!" she blurted.

Ryan put his arm round her but she was not ready for consolation. Jodie pulled away from him and growled, "You said I couldn't be a part of this stupid club because I'm an outsider. What about you?" she said accusingly. "You're not an outsider. Leah told me you were a pillar of the community. Are you a member?"

Ryan grimaced. "No. I'm not into pagan stuff."

"You know an awful lot about traditions, superstition, this Hell Fire Club and all the other nonsense."

"It's not all nonsense, Jodie," Ryan said, in his defence. "But it's a hobby of mine. It doesn't mean I practise it. People can enjoy listening to music without knowing how to play a note, you know."

"You're sure you're not a member? Because if you are…" In the heat of the moment she couldn't think of a threat that was dire enough.

Ryan replied, "Jodie, I should know whether I'm a member or not. I told you I wasn't. You have to believe me. Don't you?"

Jodie stared into his face for a few seconds and then relented. "Yes. I believe you," she muttered. She couldn't cope with the possibility that Ryan might be a traitor. "So," she continued, "because you're on my side, are you going to help me? Help me stop them doing anything horrible to Wolfie?"

Ryan smiled weakly. "To be honest, I don't relish

it at all, being ostracized from the village but, yes, of course I'll help."

"Right. There's a few things we can do. We need to plan a raid on The Olde Spotted Dog and visit the vet…"

"Hang on," Ryan put in hastily. "Why don't you just do the obvious and call the police?"

"The police?" Jodie exclaimed. "We can't do that! All our evidence is rumour or this," she said, indicating her electronic surveillance equipment. "And what I do here isn't what you'd call one hundred per cent legitimate. I could get into more trouble than Ben Godwin."

Ryan sighed. "All right. We'll try and sort it out. But let's not be rash. If we need to take a look in The Olde Spotted Dog, it's best done late tonight – after hours. It'll be the only time there's not lots of people about."

"OK," Jodie consented. "But we could do the vet's place as soon as it's dark. Yes?"

Ryan nodded, unenthusiastically. "I suppose so."

Trying to calm down, Jodie asked, "This awful Hell Fire Club, why do they do it – keep hearts in vases?"

"It's supposed to improve the prosperity of the village. That's what the old books say, anyway."

"Superstitious rubbish," Jodie hissed.

"Just a long-standing tradition. They have all sorts of rituals. I did wonder about the pig, you know.

Remember the pickled porker outside The Olde Spotted Dog? I wondered if it'd escaped from a Hell Fire Club ritual. Anyway, believers reckon such traditions have value, even if science says they're nonsense. They provide a ... feel-good factor."

Jodie was more inclined to believe that the pig had escaped from an RFR experiment at the Research Station but she didn't dwell on it. "A feel-good factor, eh? In science it'd be called a placebo, I suppose. No real effect but everyone feels as if something's got better."

"Exactly," Ryan affirmed.

"Well, I'll tell you one thing," Jodie declared gruffly and resolutely. "No one's going to feel better by killing my Wolfie!"

The day dragged. Jodie wasn't really interested in Ryan, her electronic haven, seeing anyone else or going anywhere. She wanted only to mount a rescue operation for Wolfie. Until he was safe and back in his new home, everything else seemed unimportant to her. Each daylight hour seemed interminable but eventually, the moon crept into view. The bright circle was barely distinguishable from a full moon. An almost perfectly round mirror for the rays from the reclusive sun, just a sliver of the globe had been shaved by shadow. It was a warm clear night.

"It's a pity it's not thick fog," Ryan commented. "I suggest you change into something darker. If we're going to make a surreptitious visit to the vet and The Olde Spotted Dog, I'm not sure that white is the best colour."

"Said like an old pro," Jodie remarked. "You're not into house-breaking, are you?"

Ryan grimaced. "What do you think?"

"You don't want us to smear mud on our faces, do you?" Jodie quipped to hide the disquiet within her.

"You've got to be joking," Ryan replied. "If Wolfie's in there, you'd scare him to death."

On the other side of the village, not far from the heavy power lines that bowed across the Chiltern slopes, Jodie and Ryan got out of the car and crept down the lonely lane to the veterinary centre. Ryan was feeling nervous and trembled slightly. Jodie was merely determined. The surgery was in darkness. No one lived on the premises and the late-night service had finished at nine o'clock. Behind the surgery, there was a small enclosure for the animals. Luckily, the nearest house was not in view and video surveillance had not yet reached Greenwood End. Unseen, Jodie and Ryan huddled by the front door. "You ring the bell," Jodie breathed, "and I'll put my ear to the letter box. If he's there, he'll bark like mad." As she bent down, she added disconsolately, "Unless he's muzzled."

First Ryan rang the bell and then he knocked on the door firmly but not too loudly. There was no reaction to either disturbance.

Through the flap, Jodie called into the empty

building, "Wolfie!" It was a well projected whisper but it did not elicit a canine response. She stood upright and murmured, "Oh, well. Looks like we've got to have a go at the kennels."

They sneaked to the back of the property. The animal compound was surrounded by a high wooden fence. There was an entrance into it from the house, no doubt, but there was additional access from a small track beside the surgery. Large double gates. Presumably, they enabled animals to be taken in directly by car or van. Jodie extracted a torch, hardly larger than a pen, from her pocket. Its narrow beam picked out a sturdy padlock securing the gates.

She groaned. "Now what?" she whispered to herself.

Ryan was looking up at the top of the fence. "Too tall to climb," he observed quietly.

Jodie put her hands on the fence and pushed. "Pretty solid," she muttered.

"But is it all the way round?" Ryan queried. "Especially at the bottom where rot sets in first."

Together, they skirted the fence testing the wood at its base for any signs of weakness. Inside, the veterinary patients were subdued. Only faint stirrings reached Jodie and Ryan. When the would-be intruders reached one of the sides where they came into view of the road, a car cruised past, its headlights dispelling the gloom for a few moments. Quickly, Jodie turned off the torch and they froze where they crouched. In three seconds, though, the danger had passed. The car scurried away like a frightened animal.

"Phew!" Ryan sighed. "I can't say I'm enjoying this."

"Just concentrate on the fence," Jodie instructed him.

Silently, they continued probing the perimeter. At a corner, Jodie whispered excitedly, "It's not so good here. The wood's a bit soft and worn."

"It's where the weather gets at it more," Ryan explained.

Jodie was not interested in explanations. She stood up and looked around for signs of life. Seeing none, she drew back her right foot and kicked the wooden panel. There was a crunch as the wood gave way.

When Jodie squatted down again, Ryan said, "You don't mess around, do you?"

Jodie smiled. "When something's important enough to you, you've just got to go for it. No matter what." She started to pull away the fragments of wood to make the hole big enough to crawl through. "Come on," she urged him. "Help me. We'll be safer on the inside where no one'll see us. Better than lingering around out here."

Together they yanked on the wood. Ryan lay back and pushed inwards a substantial piece of the fence with his foot. When it cracked, the hole was big enough. An entrance large enough for a couple of human beings. An exit large enough for Wolfie if he was awaiting rescue. Jodie went first and then Ryan. On hands and knees, they looked like two lame and clumsy dogs begging to get into the surgery.

Standing again, Ryan was relieved to be out of sight of prying eyes. Jodie was too engrossed in the task to be tense. "Wolfie!" she called in a hushed voice. A cat mewed and a nocturnal hamster scrabbled but there was no bark. Jodie swept the light round the yard. Beside them, there was the netting of an aviary that occupied one of the short sides of the compound. Inside it, two pure white swans sat demurely. Lame and bandaged, they were still beautiful creatures but they were no longer majestic. Injury had stripped them of their pride. Opposite, there was a holding pen for large victims. It was empty. Between, there were two rows of hutches, cages, coops and kennels. Jodie bent down by each one, flashed the light through the wire mesh in each door and peered inside. There was a droopy rabbit, a pining poodle with a leg in plaster, a hamster and a moping tabby cat. The tabby took fright at the sudden glare and made a noise that fell midway between a mew and a hiss. "It's all right," Jodie whispered. "Go back to sleep."

"No Wolfie," Ryan observed.

"No," Jodie muttered in reply. She sighed.

Ryan tried the back door into the surgery itself, but it was firmly locked.

"Let's get going," he suggested, nodding towards the gash in the fence.

"I suppose so," Jodie mumbled. Unwilling to admit that she'd failed to find Wolfie, she hesitated as if he might magically make his presence known if she delayed a little longer.

"He's definitely not here," Ryan said softly and sympathetically. "Sorry."

Disappointed, Jodie had to agree. "OK. We'll go."

They crawled back out into the immense, vacuous night and placed two of the larger slats of wood over the cavity to disguise the damage. Then, still alert, they sidled by the house and emerged into the lane again. Attempting to be nonchalant, they ambled along the lane like lovers on an idyllic midnight stroll. When they reached the car, though, they dived in and sighed with relief.

"I hate to say this," Ryan murmured, "but it won't be so easy at The Olde Spotted Dog. In the middle of the village, it's not exactly isolated. Not like the vet's. And the Godwins live in."

"I know," Jodie agreed. "So, let's go and get it over with."

Ryan parked outside Marissa's store and they walked the short distance to the pub. Twenty five minutes into a new day, the village was deserted. Deathly quiet. The front of The Olde Spotted Dog was unlit. Eroded by alcohol, even the after-hours drinkers had staggered home, more by intuition than judgement. But from any of the windows that overlooked the inn, peeping neighbours could be following Jodie's and Ryan's movements. They looked at each other uneasily.

A car, decelerating as it approached the cross-roads, threatened to catch them in its headlamps. Ryan stopped walking and embraced Jodie to hide their faces. Once the car had passed by, Jodie pulled away and teased, "Oh, you are an old romantic tonight, aren't you?" Partly, she was covering up her anxiety with bravado.

Together they plunged into the dark alley that led to the back of the pub. There was a concrete court-yard full of barrels and crates, the stench of stale beer and cigarettes and, beyond, an empty field. At the edge of the field, beech trees stood like a grim army of fearful giants, waiting for the order to attack. Jodie and Ryan poked around among the debris from The Olde Spotted Dog but there was nothing that resembled a kennel. Jodie pointed towards the back door and whispered, "Let's look inside."

Ryan frowned. "Are you sure?"

"Yes. You were sure about Ben Godwin's voice. I'm sure about checking him out."

The back of the pub was lifeless. As she tried the door handle, Jodie trusted that the Godwins had retired for the night. She expected a lock to quash her investigation but the door opened smoothly.

Ryan put his hand on her arm. "If they were in bed, they'd have bolted the door," he warned her.

Jodie paused. He had a point. But she felt the loss of Wolfie too keenly. She was full of indignation that Godwin had conspired against her dog. "They probably don't bother locking up," she argued. "Small village. Crime rate zero."

Ryan was not so sure but he followed her in on tiptoe.

Jodie's flashlight picked out the kitchen on the left. Further down the corridor, there was another room on the right. Jodie turned off the torch, opened the door a crack and peered in. It was like looking into infinity. Complete blackness. Cold. Scary. She also felt that the room was unoccupied so she flicked on her torch.

"What is this?" she muttered as the beam picked out strange painted symbols on the walls, warped oak timbers and chairs forming a neat circle in the windowless chamber.

Ryan squeezed her arm and said, "I don't know for sure but I imagine it's used by the Hell Fire Club." He shivered. "I don't like it. Let's move on. We're trying to find Wolfie and he sure isn't here."

They padded further down the hallway until, on one side, there was an entrance to the public bar and, on the other, another corridor with a closed door at the end. On the wall there was a big sign, PRIVATE.

"What's along here?" Jodie murmured. She directed the torchlight down the old-fashioned narrow passageway. Almost immediately, she put her free hand to her mouth and gasped.

On either side of the corridor, in niches in the brickwork, there were pottery urns.

"Ryan!" she cried. "You were..."

Abruptly, the door beyond the gruesome vessels opened and light flooded the hallway. Through blinking eyes, Jodie saw Ben Godwin striding towards them.

12

"What's going on here?" he thundered. "What do you think you're doing?"

"We… er…" Jodie couldn't think of anything but the truth. "We're looking for a lost dog," she said. Less truthfully, she added, "We were giving him a late-night walk in the field and we thought he'd run in here. We followed him in. I'm sorry. We didn't mean…"

The landlord strode towards them. "You're Dr Hilliard's daughter, aren't you? And Ryan Aplin. You should know better, young Ryan."

Like the trespassers that they were, they both nodded guiltily.

"After a dog, you say?" he smirked.

Rooted to the spot, Jodie and Ryan nodded again.

"Well, you don't barge straight into someone else's private property!" Scowling, Ben hovered over them threateningly. He hesitated, stroking his straggly beard, weighing up his options. After a few prolonged seconds, he decided to be charitable. "I guess it's my own fault," he muttered, "for not locking the door. I won't call the police. But don't think I'm happy about any old person bursting in without asking."

"We would've asked," Jodie said, "but we didn't think you were still up. We didn't want to disturb you."

"Mmm." Ben eyed them both suspiciously and replied, "Well, if your dog had come in here, I'd have heard or seen something. Still, let's check. Just in case. Then you can leave knowing I'm not harbouring your pet. He couldn't have got into the public bar or my quarters because the doors were shut." He waved them back down the hallway that led to the outer door. "He wouldn't have gone in here," he said, indicating the weird windowless room. "Door's kept shut." He didn't volunteer to show them the inside. "That only leaves the kitchen. I suppose a dog with a big appetite might head for kitchen smells." He ushered Jodie and Ryan in and turned on the light. Scanning the room, he announced, "See? Nothing. I think your dog must have got lost somewhere else."

"Must have," Ryan answered, keen to escape. "We'd better get cracking before he wanders too far away," he said, encouraging Jodie to leave.

"All right," Jodie said, reluctantly. She looked decidedly unimpressed with the landlord's cursory guided tour and false hospitality.

"I'm sorry we … you know," Ryan said to Ben.

"I should think so," Ben admonished. "But I hope you find your dog."

Ryan almost dragged Jodie out by her arm. Once they were in the open air again, Ben shut the door firmly and they heard him engaging a bolt.

As they walked away, Jodie growled, "How did he know Wolfie's got a big appetite? We didn't say what type of dog he is. He could've been a Pekinese, surviving on a crumb a day."

"I know," Ryan replied. "But there's nothing we can do about it right now."

"*And* I recognized his voice," Jodie added crossly. "You're right, Ryan. He's the one on the tape. I bet he's got Wolfie somewhere." With resolve, she proclaimed, "I'm going to rescue him. Wolfie's not going to end up in a pot while I'm around!"

"No," Ryan murmured. "I'm beginning to learn that you're…" He was going to say *dogged* but he stopped himself using the unintentional pun.

"Yes?" Jodie prompted, daring her boyfriend to use an appropriate adjective.

"Persistent," Ryan said, thankful for his way with words. "In a thoroughly nice way, of course."

* * *

Only three things were important to Michael Hilliard. The death of his wife, his work, and the well-being of his daughter. When something happened that jeopardized both his work and his daughter, he was bound to become heated, angry or morose. The Director of the Research Station had ordered him to take a day off to get his life back under control. Really, it was his daughter who needed to be brought into line.

He had managed to have words with the Head of Security about the Aplins. The chief had not needed to consult records. He'd grimaced, groaned and told Dr Hilliard about an incident that made Ryan an unsuitable boyfriend for the daughter of a researcher in a sensitive Government laboratory.

"Sit down, Jodie," her father ordered in the morning. "We've got to talk."

"What's happened?" Jodie asked, with misgivings.

"It's Ryan Aplin," her dad announced. "Or rather, his father, Paul Aplin."

"Oh, no!" Jodie exclaimed, guessing that her dad had dreamed up some security problem. As if she hadn't already got enough to contend with! "What is it?" she asked.

"I'm sorry, Jodie, but this has to be said. Some time ago, Paul Aplin was jailed for causing an explosion. He served a year."

Straightaway, Jodie questioned the information. "A year? That's not long. What happened?"

"It wasn't a big bomb and no one got hurt," her dad admitted. "Seems that his target was a fence, not people. Even so, it was an act of terrorism."

Jodie frowned. "A fence? What fence? What for?"

"It was the fence round the Research Station. When it was first established, seventeen years ago, there was local resistance. Peaceful protests and a few less than peaceful protests. Aplin made his feelings felt by blowing up part of the perimeter fence."

Jodie let out a long sigh and then knelt by her dad's chair. Gently but firmly she said, "As I understand it, there was a lot of resentment in the village, Dad. There still is. You know that. Destroying a bit of wire with explosive doesn't seem … too extreme to me. And I don't see what my relationship with Ryan's got to do with the security of your Research Station."

Her father shook his head. "Let me tell you about something that happened the night before last. It was discovered yesterday morning. It'll show you that the likes of the Aplins still haven't finished their protests. The fence is still a target. When the first worker arrived in the morning, she was greeted with the charming sight of seven dead cuckoos skewered on the spikes of the perimeter fence! Is that the sort of hate that you want to be a part of? They think of us as cuckoos, you know. It was a warning – a death threat in effect."

Jodie bowed her head. "That's … not very nice," she mumbled. "In fact, it's revolting. But…"

Interrupting, her dad accused, "Didn't Ryan leave here that night with some excuse about needing to get back to his mum? What did he *really* do after leaving here? You don't know, do you? That's why your relationship with him has got a lot to do with the Research Station. Like his father, he could be in on this."

Jodie was about to lose her temper but she knew that it would only make matters worse. She breathed deeply a couple of times before responding. "Yes, he *could* be involved. In theory. I haven't got an alibi for him." As calmly as she could, she added, "But Ryan isn't like that. It wasn't him. I know it wasn't."

"You don't know any such thing."

Jodie clutched her dad's arm. "Last week," she reminded him, "you advised me to follow my instincts. If it feels right to me, you said, then I'd have your support – and so would Ryan." She paused, gazed meaningfully at him and added, "I don't care what your secret policemen say. My instincts tell me Ryan's a goodie, not a baddie. Irrespective of his dad. Now I think I deserve that support you promised. And so does Ryan."

"There's more," Dr Hilliard retorted. "You're not the only computer sleuth around here. We've got them at the Research Station, you know. And they've detected repeated attempts to hack into our computer at work. A successful access by an unauthorized computer was monitored a couple of days ago. Once you were in, they could lock on to you and trace the security breach back to here. It's lucky you didn't get into any high-level programs or Security would've been straight round to arrest you. It's a form of trespass on Government property, Jodie. A serious offence. They've even had to change the fax number because someone's trying to intercept incoming messages. You again?"

Jodie nodded in reply.

"I had my work cut out, persuading the Director – Frank Granger – and his head of Security to let me deal with this," he told her. "They wanted you hauled in for questioning." Her father sighed. "Are you doing it for the Aplins? Feeding them damaging information about the laboratory's work through Ryan?" he asked.

"No!" she cried indignantly. "I was doing it for you, actually."

His face creased. "Me? How do you mean?"

Jodie hesitated. Was she brave enough to upset her dad? She felt compelled to make her point strongly. "'Some people are blinded by their own aims'," she said resolutely, quoting Ryan's definition of a terrorist but applying it to her father. "'They're so blinkered by what they believe in, they choose to ignore the consequences. They don't see the suffering they cause.' That," she said pointedly, "is how I see you, Dad. I think because of Mum, you're doing nothing to stop your research going too far. It's one thing that an RFR pulse can stun, but I think it can kill as well. And that's wrong. I wanted to find out more – to protect you from your own work. Protect you from yourself."

Dr Hilliard glared at Jodie. How could his own daughter be so patronizing? His brain registered that she was trying to help him but, after all he'd been through, he didn't need to be lectured by a mere seventeen-year-old. He bellowed, "You will not see him again!" Then he stood up and stormed out of the room.

Jodie buried her face in her hands and murmured, "Oh, what have I done?" The unravelling ball of string came to her mind once more. She foresaw her father becoming a knotted mess that was impossible to untangle. She foresaw the Research Station's third victim.

She sat and stared into her hands or out of the window, seeing little, until she had regained her composure. Then she went upstairs to her computer and discontinued the interception of the Research Station's fax messages. She found that her system had captured only one communication before the Research Station had changed its fax code. Opening the file, she discovered a confirmation of an order for a whole menagerie of animals including two poodles, two Alsatians, two rabbits, two pigs, two cows, two chimpanzees. Printing out the message, she muttered to herself, "I think they're starting a zoo." Then, she realized what it all meant. Dismally, she moaned, "They're trying to find out which species they can stun or kill!" Silently, she wondered if human beings would eventually be added to the list of experimental animals. Anyway, in Jodie's mind, the morbid memo amply vindicated her eavesdropping.

She put the hardcopy of the fax on the table in the lounge where her dad would see it and then she left the house. There was something else she had to intercept. Ryan was due and Jodie felt that it would be better to meet him down the lane than in full view of her father. She sat on a stone wall and swung her legs. It was a breathless, scorching day. While she waited for Ryan, she contemplated the pagan Hell Fire Club and the scientific Research Station. One ancient and irrational, the other new and methodical. Worlds apart but both ritualistic and cruel, slaughtering animals in the name of some higher authority. She despised both as corruptions of nature and electronics. She condemned them both.

Driving along the now familiar route to the Hilliards' house, Ryan spotted Jodie sitting on a wall. He brought the car to a halt and greeted her through the open window. She jumped off the wall and walked towards him. In shorts and T-shirt, she looked terrific. Slim but not scrawny. Agile, attractive and athletic. Her short black hair was boyish, neat and shiny. It suited her beautifully. Already he'd learned that she was assertive, intelligent and principled. Ryan could not imagine a more perfect girl. But he only needed to look into her face to realize that not everything was perfect for Jodie. In her anxious expression, there was more than concern for a missing dog.

"No sign of Wolfie, then?" he asked straightaway.

She shook her head mournfully.

"What else is wrong?" he enquired.

She ran round the car and got in. "Let's go for a walk in the wood – where it's cooler," she requested. She hardly said another word until they parked and began to thread through the trees. There, she avoided contact with him and instead prompted, "Tell me about your dad."

"Dad?" Ryan disappeared behind a trunk and then reappeared on the other side. "He's… He's a bit like you, actually. Clever, a bit bossy, dedicated."

"Dedicated to what?"

Ryan shrugged. "Anything he believes in. He doesn't do things by half. Dedicated to watching boxing and cricket on the telly. At the moment he won't miss a minute of the cricket. Dedicated to Mum. Just dedicated to what he fancies."

"Dedicated to a cause? Has he got in trouble over anything?"

"Ah," Ryan murmured, guessing what his girl-friend was getting at. "You've found out he was sent to prison for planting a bomb."

Jodie nodded.

"Did you know he didn't hurt anyone and never intended to? He only had a go at a bit of silly property. A token gesture."

"Yes. Even so…"

Ryan stopped and for a while examined the rich foliage above their heads. Then he looked into Jodie's expectant face and confessed, "He once worked in a quarry. Knew all about explosives. So, he added his little bit of expertise to the protests against the Research Station. That's it."

"Does he still protest?"

"No," Ryan claimed. "And he doesn't mess around with bombs any more. He's learned that lesson."

"Is he in the Hell Fire Club?"

"He was. Not any more. Too much of a liability with a criminal record. But … I think you could still call him a supporter, even if he's not actively involved."

Jodie shook her head sadly. "What about you?" she queried. "Following in your dad's footsteps? Are you going with me just to infiltrate the Hilliard household? After my dad's secrets?"

Ryan looked shocked. "How could you…?" He

breathed in deeply and then exhaled. "Jodie, I don't care what your dad does at all. I don't want him. I want you."

Jodie scrutinized Ryan's face. She saw honesty, innocence, exasperation and affection. She believed him utterly. She nodded and, with relief, murmured, "All right." Then she asked, "But why didn't you tell me about your dad's ... record?"

Ryan scratched his head. "I was going to. But you got in first. You told me about your mum dying in a bomb blast. It wouldn't have been very diplomatic to chip in with a father who's dabbled with bombs. Sorry."

Jodie allowed herself to be enveloped by his arms. In his ear, she whispered, "I'm sorry as well but I had to ask." She felt him nodding.

They kissed and continued to meander through the wood, hand-in-hand, not caring where they went. As they wandered, Jodie told him about her dad's revelations and the resulting ban.

"Oh dear," Ryan groaned. "Aren't you going to see me any more?"

"Of course I'm going to carry on seeing you," she assured him. "But it makes life more..."

"Complicated?"

"Exactly. And that's not all." She also told him about the ominous fax about experimental animals.

Ryan sighed. Trying to find a ray of light, he remarked, "It could be worse. All those animals, two by two. They could be preparing for the end of the world, stocking an ark."

Suddenly, they came across the sturdy wire fence that separated the public wood from the grounds of the Research Station. The fence that had seen an explosion, impaled cuckoos and probably many other demonstrations. By unspoken agreement, Jodie and Ryan approached the barrier and peered beyond it. In the distance, they could just make out the stone circle. Strangely, parked next to the pre-historic monument were three futuristic electric vehicles like golf carts. A few members of the research staff, in white laboratory coats, were milling about the tallest stone.

"What do you think they're doing?" asked Ryan.

"No idea," Jodie replied. "Can't tell from here."

"More desecration of the land and stones, no doubt."

"At least Dad can't be involved," Jodie mumbled, thankfully. "He's got the day off."

Their bond renewed, Ryan glanced at his girlfriend and then put his arm round her. "You're worried about him, aren't you?"

"Of course I am. I think he's in as much danger as Wolfie. Maybe more."

"Come on," Ryan said, directing her away from the forbidding fence and walking her back towards the car. "I can't cheer you up and I ... er ... think I'm going to make you feel worse."

Jodie twisted out of his grip to look at him. "Why?" she grunted.

"I've been thinking and there's someone else I'm worried about."

"Spit it out," Jodie said, resigned to more bad news.

"Leah."

"Leah?" Jodie exclaimed. "Is *she* in trouble now?"

"Not that sort of trouble," Ryan said. "I just... How good a friend is she?"

"As good as they come in Greenwood End. Why?"

"Her family's lived in the village for generations, you know. If something's going on – and I'm thinking Hell Fire and Wolfie, not physics now – she'll be in on it. And didn't you say she's been acting oddly? She was certainly on edge when she turned up at your house – when Wolfie was kidnapped."

"What exactly are you trying to say, Ryan?"

"She insisted that you put Wolfie in the garden before she'd come into the house. Convenient for the kidnapper, wasn't it? Wolfie outside and us distracted by a visitor."

Jodie halted and gazed piercingly at Ryan. She didn't say anything but she thought about the implications of his words.

Ryan shrugged. "I don't know anything for sure. I just... Sorry, but I thought I'd best point it out."

"What you're saying is," Jodie sighed, "when it comes to Wolfie, we're on our own. That we can't trust *anyone*."

"That's what I fear," Ryan replied gently.

"I hate to say it, but you could be right. It makes a horrible sort of logic. One thing at a time, though," she said. "First, let's go back to my place and confront Dad."

Ryan looked surprised. And alarmed. "Are you sure?"

"I'm not creeping out the house at funny times to see you. And I'm not going to lie to him every time I meet you. I don't like dishonesty. So, there's only one option left. We go back and win the argument."

Dubiously, Ryan consented. "OK," he croaked. "If you think so."

13

Ryan resisted the temptation to hide behind Jodie as they entered the house in case a missile came in his direction. He tried to be as brave as Jodie. In the event, Dr Hilliard hardly glanced at the prohibited boyfriend. He dashed downstairs and, grabbing his jacket, stated, "You were right, Jodie. I'm going into work."

"Hold on!" Jodie exclaimed. "What's this all about?"

"You *were* right," he repeated. "I've been wrestling with my own conscience. I should've listened to you earlier. I've helped to develop a great stun weapon for use against terrorists but I'm afraid, sooner or later, most new technology gets used for warfare and killing." He spoke quickly and with a passion that Jodie thought he had lost some time ago. "We've seen it with gunpowder, viruses, nuclear reactions, lasers, pesticides. I was prepared to let it happen with electromagnetic radiation because … because that way I'd get my own back for your mum. But it's wrong to kill. I'm no fool, Jodie. I've always known they were doing something with my results when I wasn't around. That fax proves it. Killing *is* on the agenda. They told me we'd finished stun experiments with different species. So what's this order for more animals? It made me want to check some files so I logged on using the remote upstairs. Recently, it seems we've received more animals than we've got in the animal house at the moment. They *are* being sacrificed. And I was denied access to some documents on RFR. Even with my password. I'm going in to see Frank, the boss, to get it out into the open."

"It might be dangerous, Dad. I don't think you…"

"I logged on, Jodie. I tried to get access to the highest level data banks. They'll already know because those files are monitored. And they'll know it was me because it was my password. If I don't go in to work, they'll come for me here anyway."

"But…" Jodie tried to object.

Dr Hilliard gripped his daughter's shoulders and said, "I'm not going to turn my back on it any more. I've decided. *You* persuaded me. I'm not having my research misused."

Jodie feared that he'd gone into self-destruct mode. "Take care, Dad," she muttered, having no choice but to relent. Her life seemed to be disintegrating around her.

At the door Michael Hilliard stopped and looked at Ryan. Then he turned back to Jodie. Demonstrating how well he understood his daughter, he guessed, "I suppose you've talked to Ryan about his father?"

In response, Jodie nodded.

"You've been as up-front as usual. And you still stick by him?"

"Yes."

Her father's eyes drifted to the carpet and then back to the young couple. "All right. I'll stand by my promise. I trust your judgement." Looking at Ryan, he pronounced, "You *both* have my blessing." He slipped out before either of them could reply.

Jodie and Ryan stared at each other in surprise.

"I guess that's one nuisance struck off the list," Ryan uttered. "And not much of an argument, either."

"No, but..." Jodie was worried about her father yet she could not help him in any way. There was no point dwelling on it or fretting. He would have to sort it out for himself. Instead, she turned her attention to another problem on the list. "Now," she announced with heavy sarcasm, "we confront my *friend* Leah."

"Really?" Ryan queried.

"Why not?" Jodie answered. "If she set up Wolfie's abduction, she'll know who's got him. If she helped us get him back, I might just find it in me to forgive her."

"But if you confront her," Ryan pointed out, "she'll go all defensive and deny everything. That won't get you anywhere at all."

"True," Jodie admitted. "What do you suggest?"

"Well," Ryan responded thoughtfully, "there is a tactic that *might* work."

"Out with it then," Jodie said eagerly.

"I could go on my own – if you trust me enough," Ryan replied apprehensively. "I could tell her that you and me, we've fallen out. Maybe I got fed up because you're more bothered about Wolfie than me. We've broken up because a dog's more important to you than me. How's that?"

Having total faith in him, Jodie cried, "Good idea. She's got a thing for you, you know. Just flutter your eyelashes at her and she'll be putty in your hands. But," she added with humour in her voice, "just be careful what you *do* with your hands. I *haven't* finished with you yet – despite what you tell Leah. So behave yourself with her."

"Promise," he responded. Then he murmured, "I hope it works because I don't think we've got much time."

"Oh?"

"The old Hell Fire Club was up to its worst tricks at full moon." Ryan glanced at Jodie uneasily. "It's a full moon tonight."

"Great!" Jodie murmured ironically. "Let's hope your tactic works, then. You'd better get going. But…" She looked at her watch and suggested, "A bit of grub first? Lunch."

Ryan thought about it and then refused. "No. I'll invite *her* out to lunch."

"You old charmer," Jodie replied, trying to put on a brave face by chuckling. She added, "If she doesn't tell all, poison her coffee, will you?" Jodie did not even stop to think if her belief in Ryan was wise or well-founded. For better or for worse, she trusted her intuition as much as she trusted Ryan. She kissed him on the lips, wished him good luck and closed the door behind him. It did not occur to her that Ryan might desert her or that, like Wolfie, he might be snatched. She went to the kitchen, doing her best to ignore the redundant cans of dog food, and made herself some lunch.

The atoms in the metal danced with such frenzy that the filament glowed red hot, emitting infrared radiation. Battered by the invisible photons, the excited molecules of starch vibrated wildly – a hundred thousand billion times every second – until many charred. Before the bread was reduced to charcoal, the flow of electricity to the filament was cut and the toast was catapulted upwards.

Burning her fingers slightly, Jodie grabbed the two slices of toast and added a layer of cheese. She slid them under the grill where she subjected the cheese to the same cruel barrage by infrared frequencies until it melted and browned.

While she ate on her own, she wondered where Ryan had taken Leah and what was happening to her dad.

The Director was getting agitated. The most significant experiment so far was taking too long to prepare. The generator was in place and working but the hundreds of sensors were not registering on the computer back in the laboratory. It was pointless to bring out the animals and connect them up, ready for monitoring, when the circuits were inoperative. The technicians were searching frantically for the fault and Dr Granger was cursing.

"Out here, I think the RFR pulse is screwing up the transmission of the electrical signals back to the computer," the chief technician said, clutching at an excuse for the hitches. "We're trying extra screening for the wires. Easy in a lab situation but these out-door tests are always a devil to set up."

"Don't waste time telling me that, Roger," Dr Granger muttered. "The trial with the sheep last week didn't play up like this."

"That was a crude stun test," Roger objected. "No animal implants. No monitors. Something we've done a hundred times before, albeit with quite a bit more power so a few died inadvertently. It still took time. It was nearly midnight before we got that show on the road. This is much more…"

Their conversation was interrupted by the Director's mobile phone. Listening to the call from Reception, Dr Granger cried, "Michael Hilliard!" Rhetorically, he asked, "What's he doing here? I sent him away today." He cursed some more and then said into the telephone, "Escort him to my office. I'll see him there as soon as I can."

Roger remarked, "Not another physicist who's proving too … squeamish?"

The Director grimaced. "I hope not. But if it is, it's my job to take care of it, not yours," he barked. Both of his last two experts, brilliant but over-burdened with scruples, had become an embarrass-ment when they found out the real aim of the project. He hoped that he would not have to deal with another conscientious objector. "Anyway," he said to the technician, "back to tonight's test. Given its nature, we can't afford to risk being seen so we'll have to wait for darkness anyway. But now we've started to set everything up, we'll have to see it through to completion, even if we're here all night," he grumbled. "What's your best estimate of schedule?"

"I know the whole point's to show the weapon works in the great outdoors – the battlefield – but I'd be a lot happier if we were in the lab for such an important kill test. It doesn't make predicting zero hour very easy," Roger explained. "I'll let you know but it looks like a long haul. Ten-thirty if we're lucky, midnight if we're not, the early hours if we can't sort out this problem soon, if we hit any more snags or if the biologists have difficulty with any of the animal implants."

"All right," Dr Granger muttered. "Keep me informed. Right now, I'd better go and see what Michael wants." He marched back towards his personal electric vehicle.

Ryan took another gulp of red wine and burst out laughing. "It's going very well," he announced. With sticky fingers, he selected a potato skin and barbecued chicken wing from the platter that he was sharing with Leah. "You played your part brilliantly," he enthused.

Leah beamed at his compliment and drank more wine. Her lips were red with a mixture of lipstick and barbecue sauce.

"And I'll tell you another thing, Leah. You're a lot better company than Jodie. She's really moping about her Wolfie. Stupid thing. A pain to be with. No fun at all any more."

Behind Leah's smile, there was a touch of regret. "It's a pity she adopted the dog, though. I mean, if she hadn't, we wouldn't have had to do the dog-napping." She tucked into a spare rib, scraping her teeth unattractively on the bone.

"If she hadn't, she wouldn't be all miserable now and I'd still be with her, I suppose. Then I'd have missed the pleasure of the meal with you," Ryan said, between mouthfuls.

Leah put down the glass of wine and chirped, "True."

Ryan topped up her glass. "Now that *would* have been a pity. I'm enjoying it."

Leah smiled seductively. "Good. I'm glad. There's lots more we could do before tonight. I mean, before we ... you know."

"Full moon," Ryan said, eyes wide. "Where will the ceremony be? The Olde Spotted Dog?"

Frowning, Leah asked, "Didn't Ben tell you?"

"It must have slipped his mind when I saw him last night," Ryan answered. "He told me it'd be OK for me to join the club from now on but he didn't go into details. He just told me about you and the dog. And what's-his-name with the tranquillizers."

"Simon."

"Yes, that's it. Simon."

"The sacrifice tonight," Leah whispered, leaning across the table towards Ryan, "you won't be able to go, you know. It's just three of us. Ben'll be in charge, of course. The Master. Then there's me and Ian. We represent the youth of the village. The next generation." Leah touched his arm, avoiding smearing grease from her fingertips on his sleeve, and murmured, "Pity you weren't chosen instead of Ian."

Ryan nodded. "Never mind. Too late. But," he added, "why doesn't everyone go?"

"Tricky," Leah responded. "The place is a bit awkward to get to. That's why."

"Intriguing!" Ryan said. "Are you looking forward to it?"

"Sure am," she answered.

"You know what's going to happen – with the dog's heart? You're not … squeamish?"

Her teeth tore the last strip of flesh from the rib. "No," she said, chewing. "I'm lucky to get the chance. I'll be glad to see the back of the dog. Always barking at me. Anyway, it's for the good of the village. I'll be like a queen."

"That's good," Ryan declared. "I just hope Jodie's not going to spoil the ceremony for you. The dog's safe till tonight, isn't he? Jodie's threatening to take the village apart to get him back. She won't find him, will she?"

Leah wiped a dribble of fat from her chin, spreading it out so that her skin became shiny. "No, I don't think so." Holding a chicken leg in her fingers, she ripped off a length of meat and popped it, end-on, into her gaping mouth. She washed it down with wine.

"I hope he's not at the vet's because Jodie was talking about raiding it."

"Simon sedated him but he didn't want to keep the dog at the surgery. Too obvious if Jodie went on the hunt. I don't know where he is but Simon and Ben'll have it under control." Leah waved the irksome topic away with her hand. "Why are we going on about this when we could be talking about anything, doing anything?" Her eyebrows rose expressively.

To distract her, Ryan murmured, "Like scoffing an unhealthy dessert."

"Good idea!" Leah squawked. She was definitely on a high. Thrilled by the coming blood-letting. She wiped her oily mouth with a napkin and said, "There's only one way to finish a meal here. Death by Chocolate." She said it with an air of finality. Like an executioner.

14

"I've got to be at The Olde Spotted Dog at closing time," Leah reported. "To receive the blessing of the meeting before we set out… Hey!" she added, "Now you're one of us, you can come to the meeting." She sidled up to Ryan and whispered, "I'd like to receive *your* blessing."

"That'd be great," Ryan replied. "Really great. But because I only found out about it yesterday, I can't make it. I promised my sister in High Wycombe I'd babysit for her tonight. I can't let her down now." He couldn't allow Ben Godwin to see him with Leah after all the fibs he'd told her. He wasn't part of the Hell Fire Club – and he didn't want to be. Next time Leah spoke to Ben, Ryan's subterfuge would be discovered. He didn't want to be around when it happened. As soon as Ben Godwin found out how Ryan had manipulated Leah, the Master of the Hell Fire Club would probably want to abandon the sacrifice of Wolfie and substitute a human being.

"Oh, well," Leah sighed. "Another time, then." She clung to his arm and Ryan did his best not to recoil.

Ryan spent some time with Leah in the afternoon but he escaped her clutches as quickly as he could – on the pretence that his sister was expecting him. Of course, he drove directly to Jodie's house.

Greeting him, Jodie asked, "What news?"

Relieved to return to her, Ryan indulged himself. "She ate like a pig," he recounted, "without the table manners. Dreadful sight."

Jodie looked at him severely, letting her expression tick him off.

"I think you'd better strike Leah off your Christmas card list," he said. "She's definitely betrayed you. I don't know where Wolfie is right now – neither does she – and, besides, he's doped to keep him quiet so he could be anywhere." Before Jodie succumbed to pessimism, Ryan continued, "But I do know where he'll be later. There's a meeting after hours at The Olde Spotted Dog. Then Ben Godwin, Leah and Ian Rickley are going somewhere with Wolfie for the … you know … ceremony."

"You mean, to kill him in some moonlit pagan ritual."

Ryan nodded ruefully.

"You wait till I get my hands on Leah," Jodie murmured gravely to herself. "You don't know where it's going to happen?"

"No," he answered. "Sorry. But it's not easy to get to, according to Leah."

"So, when they go," Jodie muttered, "we'll be right behind them. Yes?"

Ryan forced a nervous smile. "I thought you'd say that. I've got the car in case they take off in one, but I've no idea how we'd follow them without giving the game away. We'd be the only two cars on the road at that time of night. It'd be a bit obvious."

"Let's not worry about that now. We'll deal with it later – if we have to. I don't know how we'll snatch Wolfie back either. How, when and where are we going to pounce? Something else to sort out at the time. We just have to grab the opportunities when they crop up, I suppose."

"Any news of your dad?" Ryan enquired.

Jodie shook her head fearfully. "Nothing."

Three hundred and eighty thousand kilometres above them, the planet's only natural satellite was bathed in sunshine. The full moon looked too serene and distant to be responsible for the tides on Earth. It also looked too serene and distant to be the focus for myths and bizarre human behaviour over the centuries.

"Clear night," Ryan observed. "Warm and close."

Jodie and Ryan had parked discreetly in a lane near The Olde Spotted Dog and walked to the crossroads. Together they peeped cautiously round the corner of a house and watched a succession of locals entering the strangely dark pub. Amazed, Jodie said, "Who would have believed it? A quiet, ordinary English village. Full of believers in magic. Look! There goes Marissa. And Leah."

"Back!" Ryan muttered.

They both ducked out of view as a car's head-lamps flashed. When the engine was cut and the street plunged into darkness again, they dared to peer surreptitiously from behind the brick wall. Immediately Jodie gasped. It was a blue estate and Wolfie was being led from the back of the car into the pub.

Ryan laid a restraining hand on Jodie's arm. "Too many about," he submitted.

She shook off his hand, whispering, "I know." Then she added, "What have they done to him?"

Wolfie was wearing a muzzle and he walked like a zombie – without a will. Without enthusiasm for life, without fear of death.

"Drugs," Ryan reminded her. "Bet it was the only way to keep him under control."

The pub door closed, swallowing the dog and the

last of the pagan worshippers. Simultaneously, Jodie and Ryan straightened up and sighed.

"What do you think?" Jodie murmured. "Too many of them to tackle here."

"Agreed," Ryan said. "We wait. We know only three of them will go on to the ceremony. Better odds then."

Jodie proclaimed, "Two against three. Not too bad. Three against three if Wolfie comes round and recognizes us."

"That's a possibility, you know. The vet, Simon, will have him doped now but could be calculating for the drug to wear off later – before the sacrifice."

"Why do you think that?"

"Because the offering should be pure, no doubt. Untainted by chemicals."

Jodie frowned. "You seem to know a lot about it."

"Don't start doubting me again, Jodie. You know I've read up a lot about the occult, hauntings and that sort of thing," he explained. "That's all."

Jodie nodded. "Sorry. I was forgetting."

They lingered by the wall for twenty minutes that seemed like twenty hours. "You don't think they've changed the plan, do you?" Jodie whispered anxiously. "They're not … doing him inside?"

"I shouldn't think so," Ryan answered. "These rituals are carefully orchestrated. The spells don't work if they're not done just right and according to tradition. They'll stick to the plan."

Still agitated, Jodie mumbled, "What if Leah's telling Ben Godwin about what you did this afternoon? Won't that make them change things?"

"I don't think so. She'll say I don't know where they're going so I'm no threat. There's no need to change anything. And if they're thinking of plotting against me, they won't have the time until after tonight's … entertainment."

Both of them lapsed into silence as they heard the door open and the murmur of voices. They watched the villagers emerge and many disperse quietly towards their houses. "Keep an eye open for Wolfie," Jodie said into Ryan's ear.

After the main throng had dissolved into the night, Ben appeared on the pavement, surrounded by well-wishers. He was dressed in a dark gown, looking even more like a perverse Santa Claus, and he unlocked the car. A young man about Ryan's age brought out Wolfie – the anointed offering to the old magic – and manoeuvred him back into the car.

"That's Ian Rickley," Ryan informed Jodie.

Finally, Leah came out. Jodie got the impression that, even if Wolfie hadn't been muzzled, he wouldn't have let rip at Leah. He was definitely sedated.

"We're going to have to follow them," Jodie proposed.

"Looks like it. The later we leave it, the more likely Wolfie will be feeling his old self and the fewer we have to take on. But," Ryan added, "it won't be easy."

"We'll wait to see which way they go," Jodie decided, "then we'll run for your car and follow. That way, we'll be quite a bit behind them so they won't realize they're being tailed."

"True," Ryan agreed. "It's also the way we're most likely to lose them."

With Ben Godwin at the controls this time, the blue estate car pulled away and headed up the winding lane towards Jodie's house. The remaining villagers began to disband. Jodie nudged her boyfriend into action. "Come on!" Together they raced to Ryan's car and leapt in. Ryan turned on the ignition, slammed it into reverse, backed into a driveway, and then spun the wheel. He took off after the blue estate.

The road twisted and turned. Ryan yanked on the steering wheel this way and that, driving as fast as he could. His headlights picked out bends, white lines, hedges, a mesmerized rabbit, trees. He might have been closing on the estate car but it was impossible to decide. In vain, Jodie watched the road ahead for red tail-lights. Touching a button on her watch, the face lit up and she said to Ryan, "Twenty to twelve."

"Once we're past the wood, there's a long straight. If we don't see them there, we've lost them." He dropped into second to take a sharp right-hand

154

bend. "Keep your fingers crossed we don't run into any more pigs."

Jodie lurched as Ryan threw the car at the curve. She didn't complain at the discomfort. Rather, she wanted him to go faster. One tyre crunched on the debris at the side of the road. Reading her mind, Ryan muttered, "I daren't go any faster, or we'll end up against a tree trunk. That won't help Wolfie – or us."

Jodie smiled at him. "You're doing great."

Even so, when they reached the straight that led into High Wycombe, there was no sign of their quarry. They both cursed. Ryan applied the brakes and the car shuddered to a halt. "Damn!"

"You know, there is one possibility," Jodie surmized. "There weren't any turn-offs, were there? So, they must have stopped. Somewhere in the wood. They could have pulled off the road where we didn't see them."

Ryan nodded in accord and looked around for a turning place as he spoke. "You're right. They could be aiming for a clearing in the wood." He executed a three-point turn using a lay-by. "I'll go slower. Keep your eyes peeled for a car tucked into the wood."

"OK," Jodie replied. "But don't crawl too slowly. If it's tradition to do these things in the witching hour at midnight, we haven't got long." She wiped her brow free of the sweat that had begun to accumulate.

Again, the headlamps probed the road and rough kerb. Stray light illuminated the trees of the wood. But the world was asleep. Empty, devoid of life.

"I can't see anything," Jodie cried, straining her eyes.

Approaching the particularly sharp bend, Ryan brought the car to an abrupt halt. When Jodie turned to him with a puzzled expression, he said, "What's that?" He pointed through the windscreen where the beams of the car's headlights penetrated the wood directly ahead.

"What?"

"I'm not sure. It's hard to see." Ryan clicked on to full beam and then exclaimed, "That!"

There were two faint red glows. The rear reflectors of a car that had been drawn on to a rugged track that ran a distance into the wood.

Excited, Jodie exclaimed, "Let's get going!"

Ryan drove on to the track and pulled up behind the estate car, entrapping it. He turned off the lights, plunging them into darkness. They both grabbed torches and jumped out of the car. "Where to?" Jodie hissed. By instinct, they followed the trail that tapered into a narrow path through the wood. "I can't see much," said Jodie, looking all around. "I hope we're going in the right direction."

Ryan played his beam on the path, looking for signs of recent use. The ground had been baked too hard for footprints. "I wouldn't make an American

Indian at all," he mumbled derogatorily.

There was a scrabbling noise to the left and Jodie directed the gleam from her torch towards the sound. But she saw nothing. "A mouse or rat or something, I think." The powerful ray of light made the shadows of trees lie flat on the ground, like malignant black shafts extending indefinitely into the beechwood. High above them a hungry owl hooted.

Despite the heat, Ryan shivered. "It's creepy out here."

"Just normal sounds. Just nature at play," Jodie replied. She wasn't scared but she was consumed by anxiety for Wolfie.

"Hang on," Ryan uttered. "You know where we're headed, don't you?" Answering his own question, he murmured, "The stone circle! Could be. It's said to have magical powers. Maybe that's where they're going."

"But," Jodie objected, "you can't get to it. It's in the grounds of the Research Station. There's that big wire fence between us and it."

Ryan sighed. "That's true. Maybe I'm wrong."

Increasingly desperate, Jodie replied, "Well, I haven't got a better idea so let's keep going." She illuminated her watch and said, "Ten minutes to go."

At one moment, Ryan was walking at her shoulder and at the next, he wasn't. Tripping over an unseen exposed root, he yelped, "Ouch!" As he thudded to the ground, his torch rolled away from his hand, casting its light haphazardly over the forest floor.

Jodie squatted down and murmured, "Are you OK?"

Ryan sat up, mumbling at his blunder. "Fine," he answered. He reached out for the torch and then eased himself upright again. "No harm done," he mumbled. "Just bruised." Overhead, grotesque bats fluttered acrobatically, hunting insects. They stretched their membranous wings, emitted high-pitched sounds above the human range of hearing and listened with their huge sensitive ears for echoes from obstacles and prey. Their gargoyle faces seemed to twitch and strain with the effort of scanning the gloom for flies and moths by an echolocation method that was more refined than any modern military system. "Let's get moving before they mistake us for a tasty meal," Ryan said. "Besides, it must be nearly midnight."

They trudged on wearily.

No one understood exactly what had driven ancient human beings to import stones from who-knows-where and erect them in a circle on the southern chalky slopes of the Chilterns. What was the motive? What was worth all that effort? Was the stone circle a crude observatory for viewing the movements of the sun, stars and moon and predicting eclipses? An early attempt at a calendar? A burial ground or meeting place? A temple for the spirits of the dead or an enclosure for the gods? Was it for religious ceremonies? Today, the stone circle lay in the protected grounds of the Research Station and that made it the property of the Government. What was it used for now?

In Greenwood End, the villagers believed that the standing stones belonged to the people. People had built the monument, people had tended it over the years, and now people in the village made sure that the stone circle was still accessible. The Research Station's perimeter fence was not as intact as it first appeared. Once, nine days earlier, Wolfie had breached it on his own. Now three villagers pulled back the wire mesh and slipped through on their furtive mission to the stones. One of them dragged Wolfie but he was still too dazed to recognize the place that had terrified him last week. If he had been aware of his surroundings, he would have bolted.

The original purpose of the stones had been lost but they were a mysterious transmitter of energy. Even the scientists had proved that. The people of Greenwood End needed to renew that energy with a life. The scientists were planning to reinforce the energy with a pulse of deadly radiation of their own making.

* * *

At a safe distance, back in the basement of the Research Station, the Director assessed the technical integrity of the experiment. "I wish we could see what's happening live on video," he whined. "Still, it's mandatory to do it in the dark when we can be sure no one's about but I wish *we* could see what's going on."

"A non-directional pulse like this one in the open would knock out any cameras anyway," Roger reasoned. "We can screen wires but to screen a camera we'd have to encase it in a thick solid box. Not good for picture quality!"

"All computer sensors are now up and running," Kate Lawrence reported joylessly.

"The incoming signals from the animals are as good as a window on the action," Roger put in. "Still, I'd be happier if Michael Hilliard was in on this. We'd have had it sorted out a lot earlier with his expertise and experience."

Dr Granger shrugged indifferently. "I told you. I exchanged words – cross words – with him earlier. He was upset about this turn of events. He was unreasonable, neurotic and depressed. He felt he couldn't support the project any more so he walked out on us. That's his choice, I suppose. Now, let's concentrate on the job in hand. We're about to release the largest RFR pulse ever, under field conditions. No mean task. So, let's test the circuits, make sure they're fully working, one more time. We can't afford any failures."

"What's going on here?" Ben cried, as if he had discovered more trespassers on his own private property.

The stone circle had been defiled. By each of the small stones, there was a cage and each cage contained an animal. Chimpanzees, dogs, rabbits. To four of the standing stones were attached pigs and cows, too distressed even to graze. All of the creatures were covered in electrodes which were attached to their bodies and heads. Wires protruded from the cages and littered the sacred ground.

Leah and Ian looked puzzled but Ben was angry. He stomped around, tugging on his beard and moustache with one hand and holding the sacrificial knife in the other, muttering about violation of the old magic. "It's midnight but… I don't understand what's going on." He didn't know that the ritual was about to be performed, not with the life of a single dog but with a whole collection of lives. And this time Ben was not going to be the Master of the ceremony.

Attached to Ian by a lead, Wolfie began to take an interest. He sniffed the air, puzzled by the weird concoction of animal smells. He also smelled fear. With his front paw he tried to prize the horrible thing off his snout but failed. It was clamped firmly around his jaw. In his throat he formed a growl but it was snuffed out in his mouth that was kept shut by the contraption. He was confused, unable to comprehend, unsure of his whereabouts. Yet he did recognize the scent of three human beings. The girl. The one who was afraid of him. A man. The one whose hand he had bitten. And another man. The friendly one with slippers that were good to gnaw.

Jodie felt sick in her stomach. Time was running out. "I could just yell 'Wolfie!' and hope for the best."

"You could," Ryan confirmed, "but I'm not convinced it's a good idea. If Wolfie's still drowsy it'll fall on deaf ears and it'll alert Godwin that we're here."

"I know," Jodie responded. "Even if Wolfie hears, he may not be able to get away so again I'd just tell Leah, Ben and Ian that we're after them." Despairing, she added, "I just wish there was *something* I could do."

"There is," Ryan assured her. "Keep going. I'm sure the edge of the wood's up here – opposite the stone circle. I think so, anyway."

In the dark, they could have strayed a long way from the right direction and not even noticed the deviation. But something told Ryan that they were not far off course. He shone the torch on his watch and decided not to mention the time to Jodie.

Suddenly, the dark elusive shapes of birds and bats appeared above them. They were flying away as if something ahead had unnerved them. On the ground, some rabbits and mice were scattering intuitively like rats deserting a sinking ship. Mysteriously, they had sensed the impending slaughter.

"Something over there's disturbed them," Jodie deduced. "Come on!"

They ran forward towards the killing field, their torch beams bouncing chaotically in front of them.

Abruptly, they came to the edge of the wood and immediately pulled up before they slammed into the fence.

"There!" Jodie whispered. "See?"

"Godwin, Leah and Ian – holding Wolfie."

"But how do we get in?" Jodie queried frantically. "How did *they* get in?"

The moonlight glinted from Ben Godwin's knife and Jodie winced.

"There's something else going on," she murmured. "Look! Two cows and two pigs. And look at the cages. Remember the animals in the fax? It's the Noah's Ark experiment! Ryan, they're going to zap the stone circle with an RFR pulse. I'm sure they are. It's a Research Station experiment!" She was appalled. By chance, the old worshippers and the warped scientists had come together at the same time in the same place for their equally absurd and barbaric practices. Each of them seemed to think that nature and its animals were there to be controlled, manipulated and used.

"What are we going to do?" Ryan breathed.

"It could be any second," Jodie declared. "It's turning into a nightmare. A circle of nightmares. We've got to get away!"

"Do we run?" Ryan asked.

"Not without Wolfie," Jodie replied stubbornly. At the top of her voice, she yelled, "Wolfie! Wolfie! Here, boy!"

In the besmirched circle, Wolfie heard Jodie's voice. Unquestioningly, he turned and his tether drew taut. As he took off, his head jerked but he was too powerful to be restrained. Ian was too surprised and weak to stop him. Unerringly, Wolfie followed his own scent, crashed through the fence where the villagers had loosened it, and bounded up to Jodie. She embraced him and fumbled to undo his muzzle.

"No time," Ryan reminded her. "Let's go!"

"Just a second." The muzzle came away from Wolfie's nose and Jodie flung it to one side. Through the wire fencing, she shouted to Leah and the others, "You're in danger! You're in a killing experiment!" She couldn't hope to explain herself to the stunned villagers so she lied, "A bomb's about to go off. Run for it!"

In a way, a bomb *was* about to explode. A silent, invisible one.

Jodie and Ryan turned and fled like the birds, bats, rabbits and mice back into the wood. Wolfie barked with delight and galloped after them. They sprinted, trying to put distance between themselves and the standing stones.

But it was too late.

Jodie felt something sickening inside her head. It felt as if a fist had taken hold of her brain and callously squeezed the life out of it. No longer in command of herself, her legs buckled and she crashed into the undergrowth. Ryan felt an effect like a sledgehammer inside his skull and he dropped to the ground as if he had been poleaxed. Wolfie ceased to run in a straight line. Uncontrolled, he veered off comically to the left, leaning further and further until his legs tangled hopelessly and he toppled on to his side, landing in an inelegant heap. All three of them lay unnaturally still.

15

The first rays of the sun began to infiltrate the beechwood. Animals and insects scratched and scurried. Squirrels bounded across the ground, rustling leaves. In the treetops, birds made an unholy racket, welcoming the dawn. They had returned confidently to their habitat after the night of horror. They seemed to be celebrating their survival in song. At the far end of the wood, a small band of Security guards had begun to comb the area painstakingly.

Jodie's face was devoid of colour. On her cheek, two woodlice crawled. Her right eyelid twitched as a big wet tongue wiped away the woodlice and a whimper reached her ear. She issued a slight groan and struggled to move a heavy arm. She had lost all feeling in the arm so, instead of wiping her cheek, her hand slapped down clumsily on to her face and she moaned again. Bemused, her head pounded with excruciating pain. She pushed herself up on one elbow and her eyes flickered open. Wolfie licked her face again and the sensation brought her back to consciousness. Slovenly, she put her good arm round Wolfie and cried, "Oh! My head!"

Almost at once, she let go and mumbled, "Ryan! Where is he? He can't be far."

Wolfie walked away to her right, guiding her to the spot.

She clambered upright, holding on to a tree as the wood revolved alarmingly around her. She shook her dead arm to try to bring back the circulation. Dizzily, she staggered to where Wolfie was standing and whining sorrowfully.

She sank to her knees when she saw him. Ryan looked as grey as the dead. His trousers were alive with uncaring busy ants. She put her hand on his forehead but he didn't respond. She flicked away the spiders on his arm and then felt around his wrist for a pulse. She couldn't find one. Yet he was still warm. She sobbed, "Come on, Ryan! I don't know what to do." She felt helpless. "I'm not even sure if he's alive, Wolfie."

She rubbed her face with dirty hands. The throbbing in her head had not diminished and her body was riddled with aches and pains. At least the feeling had returned to her arm. She stood up and stretched, trying to force some life into her tormented limbs. Peering at her prostrate boyfriend, she sighed. She bent down and touched him again. No reaction. She couldn't feel his breath on her hand and his chest barely moved. She slipped her hand under his chin and felt his neck. "There's something here," she cried. She had detected the faint but regular beat of blood near his throat. "He's alive!"

To confirm it, his hand came up and knocked into hers. He seemed to be brushing her aside as if she were an irritating insect. His eyes opened briefly but, in the shaft of sunlight that streaked across him, he squinted and closed them again.

Jodie moved to a position that blocked out the sun. Back in shade, Ryan opened one eye and then the other. It would have been comical if he weren't so obviously hurt. He blinked twice. "Jodie?" he wheezed. "What happened?" He moved his legs a few centimetres and grunted at the effort.

"It's morning – sort of. Dawn. We're still in the wood. Not far from the stone circle." Fearfully, she looked up in the direction of the monument but it was out of sight. "The Research Station was testing an RFR pulse. We weren't close enough to be killed, not far enough away to escape. We were stunned."

Ryan complained, "My head feels like…" Under stress, he couldn't invent a suitably obnoxious description.

"I know," Jodie said sympathetically. "Can you move all right?"

"I don't want to try."

"You'll have to. You'll feel better if you do. Take it easy. Try and sit up first. I'll lend a hand."

As Ryan levered himself up, Jodie assisted by tugging on his arm. Behind, Wolfie shoved with his head. "Hey! What's that?" Ryan wailed.

Jodie smiled for the first time. "It's Wolfie. He's back with us as well. Helping. He brought me round." She stroked him, saying, "A girl's best friend. I bet his head's bursting as well but he can't complain like you and me."

Ryan lurched to one side and vomited violently, noisily. After, he glanced sideways at Jodie and murmured, "Sorry." He spat away the taste and stammered, "I feel like I did a few years ago when I drank a whole bottle of wine to show how big I was." Wiping his mouth, he added, "Never again."

"Can you stand up?"

Ryan looked up as if becoming vertical was a gargantuan task, his own personal Everest. "I'll try."

"You'll go all dizzy, I suspect," Jodie informed him. "I held on to a tree. You can use me."

Ryan put his arm across her shoulders and tottered into an upright position like a newborn foal trying to stand for the first time on feeble legs. Jodie played the part of the protective mother. "Ugh!" Ryan gasped as the world rotated in his head.

"Take some deep breaths," Jodie suggested.

"Hangovers are bad enough when you've had the fun first," Ryan grumbled. "They're even worse when there's no fun at all."

"I can tell you're feeling better," Jodie retorted. "You're beginning to chatter again."

"At least we're alive." Ryan exhaled heavily. "What about Ben, Leah and Ian? Did they get away?"

Jodie grimaced. "I don't know. We were cushioned from it by running away from the test site – and look what it did to us. They must have been a lot closer," she remarked sadly. "Can you walk?" she asked. "We'd better go and find out. I suppose we should, in case they're like us and need help. As if they deserve it after what they tried to do to Wolfie."

Feeling left out, Wolfie pushed between Jodie and Ryan to get some attention. They both grinned at his intrusion. "Let's try out the legs, then," Ryan said.

Together, they staggered towards the big fence, occasionally stopping to rest or hang on to a tree for support. Wolfie walked at their heels, taking no delight in the wood and its pungent attractions. His coat had lost its recent sheen but he looked happy to be with Jodie again.

It felt like a marathon but eventually they reached the wire barrier and clung to it. Aghast, they peered towards the stone circle, unable to believe their eyes.

Nothing. No animals, no cages. No sign of Leah, Ben Godwin or Ian. Nothing. Just thirty sandstone pillars bathed in early morning sunshine, standing and waiting as they had done for five thousand years. Their long shadows pointed disinterestedly away across the heathland. No evidence that a dreadful experiment had been conducted. No sign of modern or ancient rituals.

Wolfie refused to approach the fence at all.

"Well, it might have been a nightmare," Jodie exclaimed, "but it *did* happen."

Ryan nodded as much as his painful head would allow. "They must have done a lot of clearing up in the night."

"Does that include Leah, Ben and Ian, do you think? Were they *cleared up*?"

Ryan shrugged. Despondently, he muttered, "Possibly."

Jodie replied, "Leah may have been a traitor, but she didn't deserve *that*."

"We'd better get back to Greenwood End and find out if she's missing. I'd better contact my folks or they'll be calling the police to report *me* missing," Ryan said. "And your dad'll be worried about you, as well." With a wry smile, he joked, "Race you back to the car."

Of course, they could hardly walk. A band of three wounded returning from the war. Frequently they stopped for breath and to gather their strength.

Once, when they were quite close to the car, Jodie nudged Ryan and whispered, "Look! Over there."

"What?"

"Security guards coming this way."

"I can't see anything," Ryan replied in a hushed voice.

"They've disappeared behind a clump of trees. I think they were searching for something," Jodie guessed. "And I don't know why, but my intuition tells me that we don't want to be found by them. Let's go! Quietly, but quickly. No more stopping," she exhorted.

Ryan groaned and forced his tired legs to carry on. Together they cajoled each other into hurrying the last few hundred metres. They tramped, crashed, stumbled through the undergrowth until they were back on the track. The sight of the cars in the distance encouraged them to keep going.

"The blue estate's still here," Jodie croaked.

Ryan virtually collapsed against the side of his car. He fiddled in his pockets for the key while Jodie gasped, "Hurry. They could be here any moment."

As last, Ryan dug out the key, opened the doors, and fell into the driver's seat.

"Are you OK to drive?" asked Jodie.

"I doubt it," Ryan answered, "but I haven't got much choice, have I?" With a sigh, he turned on the ignition and reversed out of the secluded and concealed parking spot. The early morning road was clear of traffic so he pulled into the road and then started to drive unevenly towards Jodie's house. They had got away unseen.

"What do you think those Security guards were looking for?" Jodie questioned.

"If Ben and Ian and Leah were ... you know ... if they were found dead, Security would be trying to find out how they got into the grounds, or looking for their car, perhaps. Maybe they looked last night but couldn't find anything in the dark."

"If they did, it was lucky they didn't find us either," Jodie put in.

Ryan parked at Jodie's house and went inside with her. Recognizing his new home again, Wolfie began to perk up. He dashed down the hall to smell his own basket. Thankfully, it seemed to be exactly as he had left it. Jodie, though, was downcast. Her dad's car wasn't outside and he was not in his room. He was not at home. "What's going on?" she cried. "He should be here." Wretched, she slumped into a chair.

Ryan was exhausted and he followed her lead. Wolfie curled up on his basket.

Two hours of their lives were lost to blissful sleep. They were jolted awake by a combination of the doorbell and Wolfie's familiar bark. Ryan kept Wolfie back while Jodie answered the door. As soon as she saw the police officers on the doorstep, she enquired urgently, "What's happened to Dad?"

The female officer asked, "Are you Jodie Hilliard?"

"Yes. What's happened to him?"

"Can we come in first?"

Stepping into the hallway, the police officers looked askance at Ryan so Jodie introduced her boyfriend.

Once they were all sitting in the living room, the first officer said, "I'm afraid we have some bad news for you. Last night or this morning, we don't know exactly when yet, your father was involved in a road accident not far from here. Is you mother in?"

Ryan cringed and shook his head at the officers. For Jodie, he interjected, "Mrs Hilliard died some time ago."

Intent on learning their news, Jodie ignored his comment. "An accident?" she exclaimed. "How is he? Where is he?"

"Jodie, I have to tell you that he did not survive the crash. I'm very sorry."

Jodie crumpled visibly. Ryan squatted by her chair and clasped her arm with both of his hands. At first, she said nothing but then she sobbed, "He didn't survive." She seemed to have to say it herself in order to take it in. Distraught, she put her head in her hands.

Ryan looked at the police officers and enquired softly, "How did it happen?"

"That narrow twisty road. It's a black spot, you

know. Two cars going in opposite directions. They met head on. Both went up in flames."

"Are there any more casualties, then?" asked Ryan.

"I'm afraid so," the police officer reported. "The three occupants of the other car also died."

"Who were they?" Jodie queried through her tears.

"We can't say at this point. Identification hasn't been confirmed and we haven't spoken to all the relatives yet. We do know, though, that the driver was the landlord of The Olde Spotted Dog, a Mr Ben Godwin."

Jodie and Ryan stared at each other. "Ben Godwin!"

"You know him?"

Ryan said, "Yes. But not well." To change the subject, he queried the time of the accident. "You said it happened last night or this morning."

"It was discovered first thing this morning, but it's not a well used road," one of the officers explained. "It could have been first thing this morning or, more likely, it happened last night in the dark but no one spotted it till this morning."

"I see," Ryan said. He didn't volunteer what he knew about the time-scale. He was too suspicious about the whole thing to cooperate and admit that he and Jodie were in the area until dawn.

"How old are you, Jodie?" the female officer asked.

"Seventeen," she answered.

"In that case, we need to inform a guardian or an adult relative. Are there relatives? Ones who should know about your father – and who can come and look after you?"

Jodie mumbled, "Grandma and Grandad – on Mum's side – they're still alive. But they live miles from anywhere in Australia. They had to get away and start again when Mum died."

"I can stay with her for now," Ryan offered. "And my parents can put her up for a few nights."

"How old are you?"

"Nineteen," he replied.

"Well, that will do for the moment," the police officers agreed. Before they left, they made a note of Ryan's details and the name, address and telephone number of Jodie's grandparents. The officers apologized again and advised her to take it easy until someone contacted her over the arrangements that would have to be made.

As soon as the police officers walked out of the door, Jodie collapsed into Ryan's arms and Wolfie, sensing her distress, nestled against her. "Maybe he wasn't the easiest dad," she moaned, "a bit crazy, but he was brilliant. And whatever I am, he made me."

"You're brilliant as well," Ryan whispered. Then he consoled her in silence for a few minutes. Once he'd got her back into a chair, he said, "I'm just going to call my folks. They'll be anxious, to say the least. Once I've told them what's happening, I'll stay with you. I'd better phone work as well. OK?"

Jodie shrugged. "Yes. You phone. But what *is* happening, Ryan?"

Ryan made his telephone calls, fed Wolfie and prepared a breakfast that Jodie didn't want. Still, she drank the coffee. Later in the day, Ryan persuaded her to freshen up with a shower, change into new clothes and eat a light lunch. In the afternoon, when the local radio station announced that the other victims of the accident had been identified as Leah Jackson and Ian Rickley, Ryan tried to talk to Jodie about the accident. He guessed that it might help to engage her in the reasoning. Then, she wouldn't suffer silently over her dad's fate. Her grief had to come to the surface.

"I think we can work out what happened," Ryan said tentatively. "And I think you need to know, Jodie." He took one of her hands in his and explained, "We reckon Ben Godwin, Leah and Ian were killed by the RFR pulse in the stone circle. But the powers-that-be wouldn't want that to leak out. They'd want a more … palatable explanation for the public. Something that wouldn't cause such an outcry and reveal the Research Station's secrets. This morning those Security guards in the wood were about to discover the car Ben was using. When they found it, they rigged a car crash. Much more acceptable than a horrible new weapon."

Jodie looked up and murmured, "Yes. But how does Dad fit into it?"

"I think you know," Ryan responded. "You have to admit it to yourself, though. Before, haven't you been worrying that he might go the same way as the last two scientists?"

Jodie sniffed and admitted, "Yes. We know he went into work to object to the killing – the really nasty research. It went ahead anyway."

"So?" Ryan prompted.

"I guess he was overruled. I guess he lost the argument. Perhaps he threatened to quit."

Ryan nodded. "Probably, the other two scientists tried to leave as well."

"You're saying he was ... disposed of," she blurted. "But they couldn't force him to drive into a car full of dead people. They must have killed him or at least knocked him unconscious before they staged the crash."

"That's what I think, as well," Ryan said softly.

Jodie swept her hand across her mouth. "But any decent coroner would be able to tell his injuries weren't the result of a car crash." She paused and looked dismayed at Ryan. He was nodding at her. His thoughts had already travelled the same route. "But not all deaths leave a mark! You think he was out there in the stone circle!" She wept and wept.

Eventually she dried her face and said, "If only we'd known. If we'd have seen him, we could've…"

"We couldn't have known, Jodie. And even if we had, we couldn't have done anything for him. If we'd tried to rescue him we'd have only got ourselves killed as well."

"He must have been tied up, gagged or something and lain out of sight. It wouldn't have been hard in the dark."

"What we have," Ryan concluded, "is a monumental cover-up. At least, that's what it looks like." He peered at his girlfriend. She was in a terrible state but at least she wasn't brooding internally, doing untold damage to herself. She was thinking, getting angry, letting her tears flow. He put out his hand and invited her to get up. "Come on. We'll take a short walk. Fresh air."

"No," Jodie replied.

"Yes," Ryan insisted. "Just a few minutes. I think you'll feel better."

Jodie had no fight left in her. She let Ryan pull her up and, accompanied by Wolfie, took a stroll in the back garden. It was a humid day but it could not be as stifling as the atmosphere inside the house. Ryan chose not to venture into the wood.

As the afternoon become evening, Ryan persuaded Jodie to return with him to his parents' house. "That would be best," he proclaimed. "The company will do you good. You can have what was my big sister's room," he said. "We'll find a place for Wolfie, as well."

When Ryan halted the car outside his house, his father came out to greet them and commiserate. But he stopped beside Ryan's car and, with a quizzical expression, walked slowly around it. He stopped on the driver's side, tilted his head and examined the door. Then he said to Ryan, "Have you noticed your door handles, son?"

"What about them?"

"There's a lot of dust on them."

"Well, I'm sorry but my mind's been on things other than cleaning cars." He glanced at Jodie, concerned that she might think his father was unfeeling.

"No," Paul Aplin responded. "You don't understand my point." He wiped the door handle with a forefinger and then examined it closely. "I know about these things," he stated solemnly, ironically. "Believe me. Someone's been dusting your car for fingerprints. They haven't rubbed it all off. It's difficult stuff to get rid of completely."

"Fingerprints?" Ryan exclaimed. "Why...?" He stopped because he saw Jodie's face.

"Oh, no!" she cried. "I know what's happened, I think. You know those Security men searching the wood? Well, they could've found something."

"What?"

"Our torches. We forgot them. Left them there."

Ryan groaned, "You're right." Taking up the story, he speculated, "They'd have checked the torches for fingerprints. At first, they might have assumed they came from Ben, Leah or Ian. But they'd check. We know they hadn't arranged the car crash by then because we'd blocked in the estate. So, they still had the bodies. Complete with fingers. Before they rigged the accident, they could've taken prints. Later, they'd discover the fingerprints didn't match the ones on the torches so they knew someone else had been in the wood."

"They'd check me out because they knew I'd been hacking into the Research Station," Jodie proposed. "And you copped it because you were with me."

"Yes," Ryan replied thoughtfully. "Or because of..." He glanced at his dad and added, "Family history. Sometime today, they must have gone to your house, seen my car outside and got our prints off it. By now, they might know we were in the wood!"

"You'd better come in," Paul said. "Sounds like you've got some figuring out to do."

"Too right," Ryan agreed. "We don't want to disappear or end up in a fake car crash as well." Before ushering Jodie and Wolfie inside, he looked up and down the street carefully. It was empty. From now on, though, every passing stranger could be the one sent to tidy up the loose ends of last night. The one to eliminate the threat that Jodie and Ryan posed to the Research Station's operation.

16

If Jodie had been in a mood for thinking, she might have anticipated that Paul Aplin would look like a convict. In her dazed state, she didn't think, didn't anticipate anything. She simply took his offer to help at face value. He seemed perfectly pleasant and normal.

Wolfie slept in her room, at the foot of her bed. She welcomed the protection and unspoken solace that he offered. When she woke at two-thirty, she got out of bed and looked through the window at the unfamiliar scene. To the left, there were the gardens of the neighbouring properties. Some were quaint, some concreted, some wild. In one of them there was movement and Jodie flinched, ducking behind the curtain. But then she saw the dustbin shift and the fox grab something in its jaws and run away. She felt comforted when Wolfie joined her at the window with his front paws on the sill. When he barked at the retreating fox, Jodie put her hand on his head and said, "Shhh. It's OK. Only another fox."

Up above, the virtually full moon deflected the sun's rays to dissipate some of the darkness of Greenwood End. By their light, she could see that there was a field to the right where sheep were grazing peacefully. She whispered to Wolfie, "Can you hear it? A hum." It was strange and barely audible. "I bet you can. Your hearing's good. But you don't seem bothered by it. Must be harmless."

A cat jumped on to a fence below them and walked along it like a supremely confident tightrope walker. Jodie murmured to Wolfie, "Don't you dare bark, you big bully."

He settled for a token growl.

"Everything's going to change, you know," she told him quietly and mournfully. She shook her head. "No more Dad. I don't know how I'm going to... I guess Grandma and Grandad will come and sort it all out. Or maybe I'll have to go back with them. I don't want to, though."

Something quite large – a bird – flew overhead and made her jump. As she looked up towards the soaring black shape, she realized what was making the droning noise. She noticed one of the heavy cables that hung low over Ryan's house. The power line was humming to itself, throbbing proudly with 275 kilovolts. "Of course," she whispered to herself. Squinting into the distance she could just make out, at the far side of the field, the metal giant whose strong rigid arms and hands held up the thick cables. Out of her view, to the right of the house, the framework of another pylon towered above the roof. "Electromagnetism," Jodie pronounced deliberately and disconsolately. "It was Dad's favourite topic – and it used to be mine."

The next day was awful. Hot, airless and sticky. And the police requested Jodie's presence at the morgue. There was the unsettling matter of confirming the identity of her dad's body.

The mortuary was cold and clinical. Jodie was led in and everyone was too nice to her, making it obvious that it was going to be an ordeal. The casualty of a car crash lay there, covered in a white cloth apart from his head and shoulders. No matter how carefully the undertakers had repaired and prepared the body, they couldn't disguise all of the damage – and they couldn't bring him back to life. But it *was* her dad. Or rather, it wasn't. It was his shell. He no longer occupied the body that she saw. "Yes," she mumbled. "That was Dad."

She had been spared the experience of seeing death when her mum became a terrorist's victim. Her dad had taken care of it. Now, he'd taken her place on an unyielding slab. She didn't believe in life after death, and neither did her father. But her mum always trusted that something lived on. Jodie found herself hoping that her mum was right, that her mum and dad were now sharing what remained, yet she suspected that they had both been erased for ever by cold-blooded killers.

When Ryan returned from work, he drove Jodie to her own house so that she could collect a few more items of clothing. During the journey Ryan kept glancing nervously in his rear-view mirror but he did not spot anyone tailing them. As soon as Jodie opened the front door, Wolfie barged his way through their legs to be first into the hall. "No etiquette," Ryan remarked, trying to cheer her up. Wolfie's nose hit the carpet and he growled. Then he took off at speed, following some scent. He pounded upstairs.

Jodie looked at Ryan and muttered in panic, "You don't think…"

Ryan shrugged. "If he's on the trail of someone in the house, let him flush them out."

They waited for a few moments but there was no commotion and no barks so they climbed upstairs as well. They found Wolfie in Jodie's electronic den, sniffing around and glancing at Jodie with expressive eyes. He was telling her that someone or something foreign had not only entered the room but had left a smell all over it. The room had been searched thoroughly. But, Jodie realized, not by a burglar. Nothing had been stolen and, as far as she could tell, anything that had been moved had been replaced precisely. It had been a professional turning over. The thought did not appease her. She was chilled by it. Somehow, a burglary would have been less daunting.

As abruptly as he made for the computer workshop, Wolfie left it, his nose still dragging on the floor. Jodie followed him, saying sadly to Ryan, "You know what we're doing, don't you? We're following in the footsteps of someone who's been in the house."

Next, they trailed into Jodie's bedroom. She sighed. It was like having her personal space invaded. A kind of sacrilege. Then they turned round, went back downstairs and into the lounge. Jodie and Ryan watched as Wolfie traced the path of the intruder. The hi-fi unit, the magazine rack, the TV and video, the sofa. At last, Wolfie came to a halt at the book cases and he tried to squeeze his nose behind them. When he found it impossible, he started to paw the crack between the wall and the back of the shelves.

"No," Jodie cried. "You'll tear the wallpaper to shreds." She peered into the gap but could not see anything. When she slipped her fingers into the crack, though, she touched something small, round and metallic that was adhering to the back of the shelving. She yanked on it and pulled it out. She held it in the palm of her hand and stared at it.

Coming to her side, Ryan asked, "What's…"

Jodie put a finger on her lips to silence him. She placed the object on the top shelf of the book case where Wolfie couldn't get to it and beckoned for Ryan to follow her. Back in her bedroom, she whispered, "It's a bug. I've only ever seen cheap nasty ones in dodgy electronics shops but that one looks very up-market."

Ryan was shocked. "A bug? But who…"

"I'll give you one guess. I imagine the Security department at the Research Station has been working overtime again," she inferred. "There is a silver lining, though. Because they've planted a bug here, it means they're not just assuming we saw the RFR experiment and going straight for our throats. They're after evidence. I guess they want to listen in on us talking about our stroll in the wood and what we saw. If we talk about the experiment… Curtains for us."

Appalled by the invasion of privacy, Ryan snarled, "I vote we let Wolfie eat it – or bury it in the garden. Or attach it to a tree in the wood. That'll give them something to listen to."

Jodie paused and then said, "No. I think we leave it where it is. Tonight we should work out a conversation about the escapade in the wood, missing out the stone circle and the experiment. Then, tomorrow, we come back here and have a chat in the living room. Let the bug hear us. That way we're off the hook. The Research Station thinks we know nothing. No need to pursue us any more."

Ryan kissed his girlfriend. "Brilliant! I said you were brilliant."

Jodie smiled weakly. "Then all we have to do is work out how we're going to throw a spanner in their works and kill off this awful weapon – before they sell the technology to the military."

Dubiously, Ryan responded, "Sounds dangerous."

"Not as dangerous as the world would be if they're allowed to perfect it."

Ryan sighed in defeat. "I suppose not."

"Besides," Jodie added, "I owe it to Dad and the other two scientists to finish it off."

"But…"

Jodie's eyes stopped Ryan in his tracks. "I don't need reminding how they ended up," she hissed. "That's why I'm going to do something about it. On my own, if I have to."

"No," Ryan put in rapidly. "You don't have to do it on your own. You know you don't." Straightaway, he noticed one benefit of her anger. She had a mission. She was not dwelling solely on her father's death. She was becoming the wilful Jodie again. The girl he had grown to know and … appreciate. Yet he dreaded the thought that she might be hurt further.

*   *   *

Sound was not like light. While light cut through the air without disturbing it, sound was a vibration of the air. It travelled much slower than light. A word spoken by one person made its way to another by oscillating the air between. When the sound wave funnelled into an ear, its vibration made a recognizable and interpretable noise on the eardrum. The word would be regenerated. The same sound wave would also strike solid objects nearby – like a window. Just as the sound rattled the eardrum, it would also vibrate the glass, making a recognizable and interpretable noise for those with the right equipment to detect the tiny quivering of the glass.

It was easy for the Security Manager of the Research Station to plant a bug in the Hilliard's house. It had been empty – almost inviting a miniature microphone and transmitter. The Aplins' house was more difficult. There was always someone inside. The manager decided to monitor the house from outside. The equipment bounced a laser beam off a window and measured the minuscule differences between the beam sent out and the beam sent back. The differences were caused by conversations conducted on the other side of the glass and they could be translated into the original words spoken. Wind, rain and curtains could interfere with the device and it was not legal to use, but it sufficed. The substantial part of a conversation could be recorded.

In the evening at Ryan's house, Jodie and Ryan talked through and rehearsed an exchange that they would act out tomorrow in the presence of the Research Station's bug. The conversation would place them in the wood at night, hunting for a lost dog with torches, but it would eliminate any possibility that they had witnessed the activity at the monument. In the course of their chat, they would refer to leaving the wood before midnight and state that they hadn't encountered the Research Station's fence.

As darkness fell, the weather broke in dramatic fashion. Rain pelted down, converting the field at the back of the house into an instant muddy lake. Lightning flashed every few seconds and thunder growled almost continuously. The low cloud acted like a lampshade so that the whole sky glowed whenever lightning discharged within the vapour. A vast flickering light bulb above the earth. Powered by a hundred million volts. Occasionally, there was a majestic cloud-to-ground strike that was so close and powerful that it burnt an imprint in Jodie's eyes as she watched the awesome spectacle. For a split second, the night became as bright as day. The dark waving trees transformed for an instant into their natural green and then became black and eerie again. Travelling slower than the light, the thunderous shock wave buffeted the window pane boisterously.

"Wow!" Jodie gasped. She was hypnotized more than frightened by the storm. She admired and respected the absolute force of nature.

"Destructive," Ryan commented.

Jodie glanced at him and announced, "I'm glad you said that. It's reminded me of something. I know how I can be immensely destructive to the Research Station's operation! A spot of spoofing's called for."

17

While Ryan was at work, two police officers called at the Aplins' house with news that Jodie's grandfather would arrive in three days. The old man had agreed to take charge of his son-in-law's affairs, arrange the funeral and to work out Jodie's future. After the police had gone, Jodie pleaded homesickness. She undertook the long walk to her own house. It was a pleasant day for a stroll. There was little evidence of the previous night's storm. The hungry soil had drunk the rainwater eagerly and gratefully. The temperature was lower and the air was not as humid.

The Olde Spotted Dog stood like a mausoleum, closed and its curtains drawn. In its dark shadow, one small puddle did persist. Two sparrows were taking a bath in the dip in the tarmac, flapping their wings joyously and splashing water over themselves. They flew away as soon as Wolfie loped up to the same puddle and slurped up a large part of it.

Back at home, Wolfie behaved normally. Jodie assumed that there had not been any fresh intrusions. Even so, she felt unsettled. The small surveillance bug that was still perched on top of the book shelves unnerved her. It was like having a silent stranger in the house, listening to everything that she did. Spooky. Still, for the moment, she had to put up with it. She needed it for later when Ryan arrived.

In her electronic workshop, she booted the computer and checked her E-mail messages. One of them, received two years previously, she had never read. It was called *Good Looks* and it had been sent to huge numbers of computer users via the Internet, and it was unrivalled in its destructive capabilities. It contained a virus that was released merely by opening and reading the message. If unleashed, the virus would trash her hard disk, her computer processor would be placed in an infinite loop and the virus would send copies of itself to every E-mail address in Jodie's files. At the time when the virus first appeared, word of its exceptional destructive power spread quickly and most users, like Jodie, were alerted before they opened the *Good Looks* file and thereby initiated their computers' total and permanent destruction. Of course, the safest option was to delete the file at once. But Jodie had not done so. She had a sneaking admiration for the power and ingenuity of the program, and the warped creativity of its author. Keeping a copy of *Good Looks* was her tribute to its creator's brilliance. An intricate and potent program that, intriguingly, she could never access. It was like having the world's greatest, most expensive, artistic masterpiece but never being able to show it for fear of having it stolen.

All Jodie needed to do was to hack into the Research Station's computer again and, using the Director's identity, send copies of the subversive masterpiece by E-mail to all employees. In the trade, it was called spoofing. Even if she pretended the E-mail was sent by Frank Granger, Jodie recognized that she was unlikely to fool anyone into opening the door to the destruction of the Research Station's entire computer system. *Good Looks* was simply too infamous and well-known. Jodie smiled wryly as she wrapped up the virus in a new name. *Good News*. A member of staff might want to read good news from the Director. Perhaps most of the staff would be too wise and cautious to fall for Jodie's subterfuge but it only took one inquisitive person to open the file and the system would collapse irreversibly. The corruption of the laboratory's computer would not stop the electronic weapon itself, she knew, but all experimental data on it would be lost for ever and further computer-controlled tests would be impossible. The Research Station would have to replace all of its computers and program the new ones. A set-back for months. A sizeable spanner in the works.

Kate Lawrence looked at her list of E-mail messages. Two had arrived, both were from the Director of the laboratory. The first bore a subject line of *Good News* and the second was labelled URGENT. She double-clicked on the second message. It turned out to be a disclaimer of the first.

This morning, I have *not* sent any E-mail message other than this one. If you have received a file called *Good News*, DO NOT OPEN IT. It has a virus that will rewrite all hard drives, destroy their contents and mangle our whole computer network. This *Good News* document had been transmitted by a hostile outside source. Our engineers have recognized it as a version of the highly intelligent virus *Good Looks*. If this file has been E-mailed to you under my name, put your system on standby and do not use. Computer engineers are visiting each terminal in turn and will render them safe by deleting this extremely dangerous document.

Kate had liked Dr Hilliard. He'd treated her as a

colleague and not as a stupid slave. And she had seen in his eyes the excitement and love of physics. On his last day, she had also seen his disappointment and horror when he'd realized that he could not prevent the misuse of his work. Like Michael Hilliard, Kate did not approve of the recent direction of their work. She was increasingly suspicious about her colleague's fate – and the deaths of two previous physicists. Each death seemed plausible enough but, taken together, they added up to a conspiracy. They were just too much of a coincidence. Nobody employs three maladjusted or accident-prone scientists on the trot.

Yesterday, when she had raised her objections to some of the animal experiments with the Director, Dr Granger had reminded her that she worked at the Research Station under a fixed-term contract. He had made it very clear that her contract would not be renewed if she could not participate fully in the work of the laboratory.

Sitting in front of her computer, Kate had not changed her opinion. She was revolted by some of the recent research. It was time for her to care more about her principles than her salary. Soon, she would be out of a job. She had nothing to lose.

She doubled-clicked on the first E-mail message and *Good News* burst open colourfully on her monitor like an explosion of fireworks. She had let loose a virus as deadly and infectious as anthrax.

* * *

The voice–activated recorder switched itself on.

Female voice: *Coffee's on if you want one.*

Male voice: *Thanks. How are you bearing up?*

Intake of breath, then female voice: *I don't know. As well as can be expected, I suppose. Lonely. You know, Dad was hardly ever here but it still seems so … empty without him.* 3 seconds gap. *Anyway, I'll get you that coffee.*

Muffled noises and voices for 1.8 minutes.

Male voice: *Has Wolfie recovered from his ordeal, then?*

Female voice: *Yeah. Doesn't know what all the fuss was about. To him it was all a good game, romping through the wood, getting lost. Did your parents forgive you? You promised you'd be back at eleven.*

Male voice: *Well… They couldn't complain too much. I was only half an hour late after our little … jaunt, courtesy of Wolfie. You're a big bad dog, you are.*

Muffled noise for 5 seconds.

Male voice again: *It's a good job he didn't get much further. He'd have ended up in the Research Station's grounds. He must have got quite close. I don't think it's far from where we caught up with him.*

Female voice: *It's fenced off, I think. He couldn't have wandered too far away.*

Male voice: *I had to buy my dad a couple of new torches today – after Wolfie bashed into us and knocked them out of our hands.* Muffled noise. *Yes, you made us lose them, you naughty boy. They weren't designed for rough and tumble. The lights went out and we couldn't find them.*

Female voice: *At least we found Wolfie.*

The Head of Security burst out laughing. "What a performance! Rehearsed last night – luckily before the storm broke and ruined our surveillance – and delivered today like a pair of professionals. Any moment now, one of them will shout, 'Cut! It's a wrap!' and it'll be over."

Frank Granger did not feel like laughing but his lips curled into a cruel smile. After the collapse of his computer network – hardware and software all irretrievably lost – he was not in a good mood. "First, I bet it was Jodie Hilliard who annihilated our computer system and now she's staged this ridiculous attempt to persuade us she doesn't know anything." He shook his head with annoyance. "She knows everything! Her and that boyfriend. They have to be shut up. She showed this afternoon with her hacking trick that she's shrewd and out to get us. She *has* to be stopped. And I see only one way of doing it." He snarled. "Let's bring her in. She won't be expecting it because she'll think she's pulled the wool over our eyes with this bit of acting. Aplin's easy. I'm sure his subversive father could still be making bombs for his protests against us. He could have an accident with some explosives at home. Arrange it, will you?"

"It could be easier than you think," the Security Officer pronounced like a man who enjoys his work. "If she sleeps at the Aplins' house again tonight…"

Interrupting, Dr Granger cackled, "Paul Aplin could bring down the house on both of them! Two birds with one stone. Or three trouble-makers with one lump of Semtex." Despite his woes, this time he managed a broad grin.

18

Upstairs in her retreat with the door closed, Jodie whispered, "Phew! That's that done. We're off the hook. It sounded all right, didn't it?"

"Brilliant," Ryan answered. "They'll think we haven't got a clue."

"Yes," Jodie agreed. "It buys us a bit of time to work out what we're going to do next."

"I'll tell you what we're going to do next. We're going to my place and you're going to rest," Ryan insisted. "You've had a shock. You shouldn't be thinking of doing anything hasty."

"But this is my home," Jodie complained. "I feel … awkward with your parents – however nice they're being to me."

"I know, but you're supposed to be with a family

at the moment, not on your own. My folks are the closest thing you've got right now."

"All right," Jodie murmured, surrendering. "I'll come to your place again tonight but we'll talk about me coming home tomorrow. Perhaps your parents'll agree if you come back and stay with me – as long as you promise to behave yourself."

"We'll see," Ryan replied.

It looked as if a steel giant had been frozen as he strode over the small obstacle that was Ryan's house. The ogre was fastened to his ugly companions some distance in front and behind, like a procession of climbers linked by ropes on the side of a mountain. In Greenwood End, though, the spellbound walkers loomed larger than the landscape and the ropes that they carried were lethal electric cables.

Inside, Paul Aplin invited Jodie to sit down and then he gazed into her face and said, "I recognize something in you, Jodie. Let me tell you why. You see, we used to live in Scotland, before Ryan came along. Married, got a beautiful house in a really quiet place. Just what we wanted. Then what happens? The powers-that-be decide we need a dual carriageway right through it. With friends and supporters, we sat up trees, laid down in front of diggers, the usual peaceful means. The road still came." He snorted and then continued, "Ryan was on the way when we decided to move. He was born just before I got work down here. Almost as soon as we arrived, the threat of the Research Station arrived as well. No one round here wanted it, any more than we'd wanted a road in Scotland. To feel more part of the community here, I joined in the demonstrations. But I'd learned all the normal stuff wouldn't get us anywhere. We tried all sorts of skulduggery. You wouldn't believe some of it. I was still young. A hands-on campaigner. I thought an explosion would have an effect as well. Quite a few of the villagers were behind me so I brought home some dynamite... I thought I could get my way with a bomb. I didn't. I got a jail sentence and missed a year of Ryan growing up. Now, I see something of what drove me in you. You've been hurt too much. This business with your dad. Don't follow in my footsteps now because you feel strongly about what's happened. Don't let it tip you over the edge. You can't get your way through revenge. It's dangerous and futile. I tell you, your dad wouldn't thank you for it. He *can't* thank you for it. You should be grieving, not plotting. I'm worried about you."

Jodie fought to hold back her tears. "Thanks," she stammered. "But you don't have to worry about me. I'm not after revenge – only justice. I'm fighting to stop a weapon, not to make one."

"Just be careful how you fight," Paul advised her. He got up and left the room.

Ryan stared after his father and then turned to Jodie. "That was quite something," he declared. "He's never wanted to speak about it before. He's never opened up like that with me. You're privileged."

Jodie nodded in reply. "But I still have to do something. I can't just let it go."

"Think about it, Jodie. He's got a point. He knows."

That night there was no storm to keep Jodie awake, but she lay in bed and stared into the darkness. Something was not allowing her to sleep. Her thoughts, the foreign noises, the hum. In her own house, she was familiar with all of the creaks and groans and bumps that sounded in the night. Only the odd ones would disturb her. In an alien house, all of the noises were odd. She couldn't distinguish the natural harmless ones from the ominous.

But Wolfie could.

At one-thirty, the ever vigilant wolfhound made Jodie jump and cry out in shock as he suddenly emitted a loud ill-tempered bark. He dashed to the door and scratched at the wood.

Her heart still in her mouth, Jodie turned on the bedside light and said, "Wolfie! What *are* you doing? Calm down. You'll wake up the whole neighbourhood."

Ignoring her, Wolfie continued to growl, bark and claw at the door.

"All right," she grumbled. "I'll come with you."

As soon as she opened the door, Wolfie scampered out and headed for the stairs.

Jodie jolted again as she almost knocked into a figure on the landing.

"It's only me," Ryan whispered. "What's wrong with Wolfie? He woke me up. Nearly brought the house down. What's got into him?"

"I don't know. He went downstairs."

"Like an express train," Ryan commented quietly.

"Well," Jodie said, "Wolfie's judgement is pretty good. I think I'd better go down and find out what's going on."

Ryan switched on the landing light and said, "Me, too."

Together they padded down the stairs, the carpet deadening the sound of their footsteps. Wolfie was not in the hall but the kitchen door was wide open as if he'd barged through.

"I hope his stomach hasn't got the better of him again," Ryan mumbled.

After a few seconds of flickering, the fluorescent light glowed harshly. Wolfie was sitting by the side of the table, resting his chin on the surface and whimpering. But it wasn't a bone or chocolate or other treat out of his reach on the table top. There were four metal pipes, plugged at each end, with wires poking out of them. It looked as if a small child had been let loose with tubes, plasticine, straws and a digital clock.

Ryan peered at the device with his mouth open.

Jodie cried, "What on earth…?"

Ryan turned to her, his face drained of colour, and spluttered, "I'd better get Dad."

"It's not what I think it is, is it?"

"Yes," Ryan croaked. "I think it's a bomb."

Not daring to move, Jodie could hardly take her eyes off the dreadful gadget. Four pipes packed with potential energy, waiting to be released. She ordered Wolfie to her side. "Come away, boy." Rooted to the spot, she was convinced that the bomb was meant for her. But, if it was, the Research Station could not have fallen for their ploy. Somehow, Frank Granger and his uncompromising security staff had discovered that she and Ryan knew about the secret weapon, the test at the stone circle and the cover-up of the deaths. And now the authorities were aiming to silence them for good.

At the bottom of the stairs, Ryan screeched, "Dad! Dad!" Answering the murmuring from his parents' bedroom, he called, "You'd better come down and take a look at something in the kitchen!"

Paul came down the stairs in his dressing gown. Ryan's mother followed more slowly and dreamily.

When he saw the device on the table, Paul's eyes widened with fright and suddenly he clicked into gear. "Ryan," he commanded, "take your mum and

Jodie out. Front door. Go behind next door's house. Far side. Now."

"What about you?" Mrs Aplin cried.

"I'm not letting this thing blow up our house!" Paul flexed his fingers. "I can deal with it. Defuse it as soon as you're clear. You have to go. Now. All of you. It's on a timer. It could go off any moment." He smiled reassuringly at his wife. Then he glanced at Jodie with a kind expression and said, "Be careful. You've chosen to take on some ruthless people." Clearly, like Jodie, he believed that the bomb was the work of the Research Station.

It wasn't cold outside but in nightclothes it seemed chilly. They shivered. Only Wolfie seemed immune. He looked puzzled but pleased to be in the fresh air. Ryan's mother was numb with fear. Ryan seemed bewildered but remained composed enough to lead the small band of deserters away from the danger. Jodie was blaming herself. The Aplins had offered her shelter and in return she'd placed them all in danger.

"This way," Ryan breathed, directing them along the pavement in front of the house next door. But he wasn't fast enough. And Paul Aplin failed in his attempt to defuse the bomb.

Before they could reach the safety behind the house next door, there was a huge explosion that sounded like the end of the world. The pressure boomed in Jodie's ears and emptied her stomach instantaneously. It picked her up like an unwanted doll and threw her to the ground. Fragments of shattered glass shot like bullets from every single window in the house. A deadly white shower of sharp splinters. Roof tiles flew upwards and then rained down on Jodie, Ryan and Mrs Aplin. The tiles smashed as they clattered to the ground. Particles of plaster filled the air like white smoke. Doors and frames were wrenched from their fixtures and fell away. The fence at the bottom of the garden blew outwards like a sail and then collapsed. Above Jodie, the power lines bowed upwards like skipping ropes propelled by overenthusiastic girls. At the insulator where one of the lines was attached to the pylon, the ferocity of the whiplash severed the cable. In a shower of sparks, the thick wire snaked and plummeted like a formidable, frightful firework. Mrs Aplin shrieked. Crackling and burning everything it touched, the electric cable thrashed about like a wild and powerful serpent's tail, searching for a way to earth. It contacted a small bush in their neighbour's garden. The shrub lit up like a Christmas tree and smouldered. In its death throes, the snake flopped on to the lawn and slithered threateningly. It dipped its tail in the pond, sizzled and lay still, exhausted and harmless.

The aftermath of the blast was a dreadful silence. Or perhaps the explosion had deafened Jodie. Shredded curtains and blinds dangled pathetically out of the wrecked windows. The ground was littered with rubble. A door twisted on its remaining hinge and then succumbed to the inevitable. It hit the ground and sent up a cloud of debris. Jodie tasted dust and blood in her mouth. Suddenly, she felt something touch her back. She twisted and saw Ryan. He had a gash on his cheek, a brown stain down his front and he looked drunk. But he wasn't. Just dazed. "Are you all right?" he slurred.

Jodie grunted, "I think so."

She didn't remember much about the next hour. She was aware of people rushing out of nearby houses. Blue lights flashing. Being placed on a stretcher. A journey. A doctor shining a light in her eyes and nurses dressing wounds. An injection and pills. There was a policewoman asking questions and a whisper not meant for her. "Aplin up to his old tricks again." She did recall asking about Ryan, his mum and Wolfie. If she heard the answer, it didn't register in her brain.

She became fully conscious when Ryan visited her in the hospital ward. He had a dressing on his cheek, another on his neck, and a black eye. He was saying something about a piece of flying glass having missed his jugular vein by a centimetre.

"Your mum?" Jodie queried.

"Broken arm. Cuts. A bit of glass punctured her lung. Shock. They're keeping her in but she'll be OK, they say."

Jodie nodded, relieved.

"You and me, we'll be discharged as soon as the doctor comes round and checks us out."

"Do you know what happened to Wolfie?"

"Someone called in the vet. That's all I know."

"The vet!" she cried. "But he nearly..."

"That's all over, Jodie. I'm sure he'll do what he can for Wolfie now."

Jodie grimaced but accepted Ryan's word. She hesitated before she asked, "What about your dad?"

Ryan looked away, shaking his head.

Jodie and Ryan were back on their own in Jodie's house. They didn't have a choice of homes any more. When Jodie glanced in the hall mirror, she groaned. Her face showed several grazes and her lip was fat with blood and bruising. An ugly scab was forming. No more kissing for a while. One side of her face was an unhealthy purple. She looked as if she had just gone ten rounds with the champ. On top of that, she felt sore all over. The painkillers could only do so much. Her left arm was patched up where a chunk of masonry had hit it. Her right leg was bandaged where it had been speared by glass.

Jodie limped to the bookshelves, snatched the bug and dropped it on to the floor. She was about to stamp on it when she had second thoughts. Her leg was too tender to deliver the crushing blow that the bug deserved. Besides, a really hefty thud would only drive it into the soft pile of the carpet. Instead, she picked it up and, together with Ryan, went out into the back garden. There, she threw it ceremoniously and vigorously, banishing the listening device to the wood. It felt like exorcizing a troublesome ghost from her life and her house.

Back inside, Jodie said, "I'm sorry about your dad, Ryan. It was all my fault."

"That's not true," Ryan replied. "It was the Research Station and that electronic weapon. It was *their* fault. Not yours."

For a while they hugged each other in shared misery and sympathy. Ryan sobbed on her shoulder and she held him tight. The moment was broken by the sound of a letter being delivered and slapping on to the doormat. Slowly, they disentangled themselves and Jodie went to fetch the mail from the hall.

The envelope was addressed to Ms Hilliard and the letter itself was not signed.

Dear Jodie,

You don't know me but, in a way, I know you. I was a colleague of your father and I admired him a lot. At work, your dad often spoke about you. He was very proud of you. Apparently, you are gifted with computers and all things electronic. I wonder if that means you sent some good news to the Research Station recently. If so, it means you do not believe the official version of your dad's death and you are looking for a way of exposing wrongs. You are right to be suspicious about your dad's "accident".

Now the Research Station does not have a working computer system, many of its security features are not in action. They have had to revert to old access numbers to operate locks on doors. You may be interested to know that the back door of the laboratory block is accessible from the grounds. Punching in the number 53143 will give access to the RFR laboratory. It's down in the basement on the left. I wonder if this information is useful to you. If you were to act on it, you would still have to contend with video surveillance inside the building. I don't know how.

The letter ended abruptly and Jodie read it again before handing it to Ryan.

At first, Ryan did not volunteer an opinion on the message. Understandably, he was more worried about his mother and upset by the death of his father.

Jodie was more excited. "It's like being given the key to the door!"

"So what?" Ryan muttered. "What can you do?"

"If I got in, I could ... I don't know ... sabotage the weapon."

"They'll just make another one. You can't stop it."

Jodie paused and then responded, "Maybe destroying the weapon won't stop the project. I agree. But destroying the credibility of the Research Station would. If I got in, I might be able to rig something that they couldn't cover up. If people knew about it – and if the truth about Dad and the others got out – they'd be closed down."

Ryan sighed. "But how would you do it? And how would you deal with the video cameras?"

Jodie's enthusiasm waned. She didn't have a plan. The code number was a means to an end but she had no clear idea how to bring it about.

"On top of that, it could be a trap," Ryan warned her. "Maybe someone's trying to draw you in so they can have another go at getting rid of you."

"I don't think so," Jodie replied. "This must have been posted yesterday. Then, they'd be expecting the bomb to do their dirty work so they wouldn't be setting up a trap as well. I'm sure it's genuine, and I ought to make use of it. I'll think about it."

Ryan groaned. He'd learned that there was no point arguing with Jodie once she'd got her sights fixed on a target. But this! It was ridiculously dangerous. He had to admit to himself, though, that it would be immensely gratifying to strike a devastating blow against the institution that had murdered his father.

As soon as it was ten o'clock, Jodie phoned the veterinary centre. Her conversation with Simon was strained. She could not forget that, a few days ago, the man now treating Wolfie was collaborating in a plot to sacrifice him.

"Some substantial pieces of flying glass embedded in his front left leg," the vet reported. "I operated straightaway and removed it all. You'll be pleased to know he'll make a full recovery. In fact, you can come and pick him up. He's not happy here. He'll recover better at home."

Jodie was anxious to collect Wolfie straightaway so Ryan offered to take her. His car looked as if it had been driven through a war zone. The roof and passenger's side had been dented by shrapnel from the explosion. Luckily, though, the windows had remained intact. It was safe to drive even though it was battered and abused.

Wolfie looked similarly battle-scarred. His left leg was wrapped tightly in a bandage and he seemed a little groggy. Even so, he bucked up when he saw Jodie and Ryan.

"He'll hobble for a while but a bit of walking won't do him any harm. He'll refuse to budge if it gets too much for him." Simon did not seem to be ashamed of his part in the doomed ceremony at the standing stones. He could still look Jodie in the eye. "I'll need to see him again in a week. Then he should be fine. He's a lucky dog."

"Lucky?" Jodie cried.

"His injuries could have been a lot worse. Glass could have pierced vital organs. And, er, he might not have escaped the car accident up by the wood."

"Car accident!" Jodie blurted out.

"Yes. You know. Your father, Ben, Leah and Ian. We share a common grief. I ... regret it very much."

His sudden pained expression told Jodie that he was feeling genuine remorse, but only for his fellows in the Hell Fire Club, she thought. He also seemed to believe the official version of the deaths. She took the opportunity to enlighten him.

Throughout Jodie's account of the true events in the grounds of the Research Station, Simon's mouth remained open with surprise and shock. At the end, he uttered, "That's outrageous!" He paused before adding, "What are you going to do about it?" He asked the question as if there was no doubt in his mind that something had to be done.

Ryan grimaced as Jodie said, "I'm going to get into the laboratory and somehow sabotage the operation. I've got a key to get in from the grounds."

Simon responded, "You want to stop the weapon development and close down the lab. I'm sure the ... villagers will throw their weight behind you. We want to reclaim that land. We share an aim. We should pool our efforts. There's a meeting tonight. I can tell them what you've told me and I'm sure they'll agree to help. For a start, we can show you a way into the grounds near the stone circle."

"Let's be up-front about it," Jodie said. "We're talking about the Hell Fire Club, aren't we? If a good few members would turn out, there's more you can do than lead me into the grounds. You might be able to buy me a little time." She explained, "You could mount a protest against animal experiments – in full view of the video cameras. While you distract the guards, I could break away and get into the lab." Once in, Jodie thought, she'd be able to weave her own particular electronic magic in an attempt to renew the world. There, she'd make any sacrifice necessary to halt the progress of the RFR weapon.

For a few seconds, Simon was silent. Then he said, "I'm not sure I can sell it to the Club quite like that. You have your methods. The Club has its own, more … traditional ways. I'm not sure the members would want to be relegated to the role of decoys. We have powerful cleansing methods of our own. But, as I said, we should pool our efforts. Help each other. Leave it to me to persuade the villagers. I'm sure we can sort something out."

Jodie amazed herself. She had initiated an unlikely alliance with the Hell Fire Club.

After lunch, Jodie played nurse to Wolfie and Ryan returned to the hospital to comfort his mother. It was ironic that, after years of working with explosives, followed by imprisonment and rejection of direct action, Ryan's father had succumbed to a bomb. "It's crazy," Ryan said to his mum softly.

"After Dad had turned his back on it…"

"It's a miracle it didn't happen before," his mum sobbed. "Every day, I used to live in fear of him blowing himself up at the quarry, but he never did. Then, when the cuckoos came, he dabbled at home. I was petrified but I couldn't stop him. He was determined. And look what happened. No good came of it but at least he was safe. Now this! I can't believe it." In her distress, her whisper became almost inaudible. She touched her son's arm weakly. "He was a wonderful husband and father. There's a lot of him in you, Ryan. Now he's gone, don't try and take the law into your own hands. Don't you copy your dad. You and me, we both have to work out a way of coping without him. It won't be easy but violence isn't a way of doing it, I'm sure."

Together, they wept.

Once, the room in The Olde Spotted Dog, with its old oak beams and fanciful symbolic decorations, seemed scary. Now, with an electric light glaring and the villagers sitting attentively in a semi-circle, it was as mundane as a classroom. So ordinary that Jodie could almost forget that it was midnight and Ryan could overlook the fact that he had been asked to leave the hospital two hours ago. It was the witching hour but the assembled villagers did not look like witches. Everything but the occasion was commonplace.

At the front Simon was like a teacher, explaining to the gathering what Jodie had told him and why there were two non-members among them. He stressed the horror of how their friends – Ben, Ian and Leah – had really died. When he'd finished, there were a few questions which Jodie did her best to answer. Once she'd had her say, she was ordered to leave the room with Ryan and wait for their verdict.

Inside, unbeknown to Jodie and Ryan, the cries of indignation were loud and insistent. "Help the daughter of a cuckoo? Never!"

Simon waited for the abuse to die down and then argued, "Remember, the real cuckoos killed her father."

"That's what she says," someone called. "He could've driven into Ben's car and killed him. Along with Ian and Leah."

"I don't think she's lying," Simon countered. "Think of Paul Aplin as well. We owe it to him. He came here and did his best to help us. He became one of us. And he went to prison for our cause." No one disputed this line of reasoning, so Simon continued, "But we don't have to go along with everything the Hilliard girl wants. We tell her we will. But … we have our own agenda. She can be a decoy for *us*. Let's face it, she doesn't have a hope of stopping anything on her own. She doesn't matter. Just a kid against the whole organization. We need to call on the life energy, the ancient powers, to cleanse the land and the stones. It's the only way. We continue what Ben started. We tell the girl we'll help her, then, while she's occupying the guards, we enact the final part of the cleansing. *That's* the most important thing."

Jodie was called back into the stuffy windowless room. Apparently with one voice, the villagers offered to do what Jodie asked. Tomorrow night, at the agreed time, they would lead Jodie into the grounds of the Research Station and, for the benefit of the security guards, hold a decoy protest to buy Jodie as much time as they could.

Nudging her, Ryan said, "I'm coming too." He'd decided that his dad did not deserve such a swift and deceitful death. He did not deserve to take the blame for his own demise. Ryan had to act. "Mum told me not to use violence, that's all," he explained. "She didn't say anything about trespassing."

"Are you sure you want to come?" she asked him.

"Certain."

Jodie smiled at her boyfriend. "Thanks. It'll be good to have you on board. Are you any good with aerosol paint sprays?"

Looking surprised, Ryan said, "You don't want to vandalize the place, do you? Daubing stuff on the walls?"

"No," Jodie answered. "I've got something else in mind."

19

Ryan stood outside the devastation that had once been his home. Now it was a bomb site. Builders had moved in to make the property safe and forensic scientists dressed in white overalls were combing the scene of the crime but he was kept out. He had no idea if his belongings were still in his room or whether they had been ravaged by the bomb and strewn all over the place. Overhead, electricians were repairing the power line. Ryan was pleased only that his mother, still in hospital, did not have to see the destruction until she was better.

He nearly jumped out of his skin when he felt a hand on his shoulder. "Sorry," a neighbour mumbled. "I just wanted to ask if you were OK."

Ryan nodded. "Thanks."

"And your mother?"

"She's recovering in hospital. They say she'll be fine but…" Ryan shrugged. He decided not to discuss his mum's state of mind with a man who felt compelled to do his neighbourly duty.

"I'm sure they're looking after her well."

"Yes."

The embarrassed resident concluded, "You're welcome to come to my place if you need anything."

"Thanks," Ryan repeated. He was grateful when the man retreated. It was a time for being on his own.

Even though the clothes that he now wore fitted him reasonably well, they did not feel comfortable. They were not his and there was something disturbing about wearing a dead man's clothes. But he had no real choice. He couldn't get to his own wardrobe and, even then, he might have only tatters. This morning, after a sleepless night in Jodie's house, she'd offered him the pick of her father's clothing. Ryan had refused at first but soon realized that he would have to accept the offer.

Lingering outside the ribbon that fluttered around the house, Ryan cried. He cried because of his father, because of his injured mother, because Michael Hilliard's clothes were available. And because of Jodie's kindness and support. His emotions were as disordered as his house. But he was sure of one thing. He felt that something bigger than the Research Station and the Hell Fire Club was at work. It *had* to be. There had to be some sense behind this mess. He wouldn't voice his opinion to Jodie because he thought she'd scoff at the idea. He had no evidence for it but he believed in it. Whatever it was.

Suddenly, he knew that he was doing the right thing. Tonight he would be beside Jodie.

Marissa looked up at her customer and mumbled, "You know what they say about bad luck, don't you? Always comes in threes, it does. First there's this car accident — that wasn't an accident at all. Then there's the explosion that killed Mr Aplin. Not his own making, it seems. So, what's the third bit of bad luck?"

"Are you saying we shouldn't go tonight?"

Sensing a reprimand in the customer's tone, Marissa hesitated. "No. I'm not saying that — not exactly. I'm just erring on the side of caution. That's all. Number three's just around the corner and I don't want to tempt fate."

"But everyone's blood's up — especially after poor Ben, Leah and Ian. You know."

"Yes. Like everyone else, I was all for it last night," Marissa whimpered, "but in the cold light of day…"

A crisis could make both heroes and cowards. Most of the members of the Hell Fire Club were so incensed that they were determined to awaken the ancient power and purge the Research Station from their land. There were more willing volunteers than the ceremony required. Only the most dedicated and courageous were needed.

Jodie spent the day quietly at home with Wolfie. She had plenty to think about. Dad – who had left unfinished business. Ryan – who disconcerted her with his face like a damaged boxer and clothes from her father's wardrobe. Mrs Aplin – who would soon need lodgings until the condition of her own house was clear. Tonight's raid – where she would try to undermine the development of an RFR weapon that was well outside her range of knowledge. She wished that she had a clear plan but she feared that she would have to make it up as she went along. At least she'd have Ryan with her.

She took Wolfie for a short stroll in the wood. She limped and he hobbled. They both enjoyed the fresh air and exercise, even if it was slightly painful. Jodie was determined that her superficial wounds would not get in her way tonight. She was less sure about Wolfie. It had not occurred to her that she should leave him behind at home. Wolfie was her family now. He had a right to be part of the evening's proceedings. She liked to think that even an injured Wolfie would want to be with her. She hugged him, saying, "You're a brave dog, aren't you? You want to come. Your walking's not too bad. I think you'll make it OK. Won't you, Wolfie? You'd prefer to suffer a bit with me than be here on your own, wouldn't you?"

Wolfie yapped happily. It could have been a "yes".

The walk had inspired Jodie. She worked out a scheme that might be a safety net if everything went wrong tonight. Cheered, she spent some time in her retreat tinkering on the Internet.

It was time. Jodie and Ryan mixed with the fifteen most vengeful villagers. Plenty to make a sizeable diversion, Jodie thought. And they were straining at the leash. Eager to see the demise of the Government laboratory. She tapped Ryan's shoulder and breathed into his ear, "It'll be all right, Ryan. Lots of support for us." The small convoy of five cars made it's way along the tortuous road to the track near the stone circle. One by one, they pulled into the wood, came to a stop and extinguished their lights. There was no turning back now. The gloomy beechwood consumed them. A cold ominous wind rustled the foliage.

In Ben's absence, Simon took charge of the Hell Fire Club. Several of the members carried torches. Once more, flashing beams of light pierced the wood, attracting insects and scaring away nocturnal animals. Jodie held Ryan's hand as they walked behind the small band of pagans. To make sure

Jodie and Ryan didn't draw attention to themselves, they were dressed in black clothes and Jodie kept her torch hidden. Beside them, Wolfie padded gingerly. He did not scamper around following scents. He recognized his own limitations. He seemed to know that he had to preserve energy and protect his wounded leg.

Before long, they were out of the wood and at the perimeter fence. "It's just up here," Simon whispered, directing his torchlight to their right. "Come on."

At one point, Simon knelt down. The wire mesh was attached to the supporting post by discreet hooks. Some time ago, it had been cut but the fastening at the post disguised the damage. A slight tug and the fencing pulled away. On his hands and knees, Simon crawled through the gap. As quickly as they could, the bold followers of the old ways did the same. When it came to Jodie and Wolfie, bringing up the rear, the wolfhound balked at the prospect. He was remembering his last two visits to the stone circle. He looked dubiously at Jodie.

Jodie patted him on the back. "It's all right this time," she said soothingly. "I won't let anything happen."

Wolfie still hesitated.

"Go on," Jodie murmured, pushing his backside. He refused to budge.

Ryan came back through the hole and suggested,

"You go through. He'll follow you. I'll stay back till he does."

"OK."

When she was on the other side of the barrier, she stood up and said, "See. It's safe. Come on."

Reluctantly, Wolfie put his head through the gap and smelled the air, testing it. He did not sense any danger so he carried on.

"Good boy," Jodie encouraged him.

Even when he was beside Jodie and joined by Ryan, Wolfie seemed wary. His tail drooped and his eyes and nose would not rest. Alert, he sniffed and scanned the heath constantly.

Jodie hoped that she had not misled Wolfie by telling him that he was not in danger.

Without a word, the band of trespassers crept past the thirty stones. Over the hundreds and thousands of years the rocks had witnessed all manner of human antics. Sacrifices, dances, observations of the seasons, burials, silent worship, plays, scientific studies. They remained aloof. Immune to it all. If they could wear an expression, it would now be one of reproach. Their patience with puny, short-lived humans would be growing thin. If they had a choice, they would sweep away all those responsible for the foolishness. The narrow shaft of light from Simon's torch picked out the tall, pitted stone, permanently on guard at the circle of nightmares. It ignored the attention. Whatever happened to the meagre mortals, looking serious and self-important as they hiked across the heath this night, the timeless stones would be unaffected. They would still be there in ten thousand years. Still inert, still unsympathetic to the human folly around them.

In the distance, the buildings came into view. They glowed eerily under security spotlights. Above them, the moon gleamed brightly in an infinite black sky at one moment and in the next it was obliterated by ugly black clouds. By unspoken agreement, the intruders halted for a few seconds, surveyed the ominous premises and shuddered. The breeze had brought an uncomfortable chill to the summer air. Behind them, birds and bats fluttered over the dark roof of the wood as it swayed and sighed in tune to the wind. Some inner voice told the creatures to take flight. Humans no longer listened to the same voice. The night reeked of menace.

20

The Head of Security looked up at the turbulent sky and felt a twinge of foreboding. He didn't know why and he told himself not to be absurd. Just a heavy atmosphere. Perhaps a storm on its way. As he looked at the broken circle of the moon, it suddenly disappeared. Not a cloud obscuring it this time but hundreds of bats setting out on a communal hunt. He trembled, then frowned and shook his head. It's only natural, he mocked himself. Even so, he called out to a couple of his staff, "It's a funny night. You two do an extra patrol of the grounds. We don't want any more trouble. Keep in touch."

Mumbling curses, the two weary guards set off all over again.

*   *   *

"This," Simon announced abruptly, "is where we leave you. We wish you good luck."

"Here?" Jodie exclaimed. "In the middle of the field? But you agreed to create a diversion." She pointed towards the bland concrete of the Research Station that was brought to uncanny life by security illumination. "Up there."

"We got you in, guided you this far. From here you can see where you're going. And we *are* going to help each other, as we agreed. While you go on, we're going to mount our protest, our cleansing, here at the circle where we can summon the energy of the stones and direct it at the Research Station."

"But that's..." Shocked at being let down, she felt like insulting the members of the Hell Fire Club. She stopped herself because they might have turned round and marched back to the village, leaving her totally in the lurch. "I need someone to distract the security guards!"

Simon addressed her as if she were a stupid little child. "Believe me, summoning the supernatural, the wrath of the stone circle, is the most potent assistance we can offer."

Jodie let a long sigh escape her lips. There was no such thing as the supernatural, she believed, only nature. And nature was not for humans to dictate. But it wasn't the time and the place to argue. Disgruntled, she muttered tersely, "Thanks for getting us this far." She turned to Ryan and said, "Come on. We'll get the job done on our own."

Taking a deep breath, Jodie and Ryan pushed on, towards inevitable confrontation. With Wolfie, they looked like a tiny, lame and improbable army invading an impregnable fortress. They trudged up the slight slope and came to a halt at the edge of the darkness. "Well," Jodie whispered, "this isn't what I had in mind. I hoped the Hell Fire Club would be protesting in front of the cameras and Security would be rushing about all over the place, arresting them, not paying us any attention. Obviously I hoped for too much."

Ryan replied glumly, "It looks like *we're* diverting the guards for the Hell Fire Club instead."

"Yeah. But… We've come too far to give up at the first sign of trouble." Really, she couldn't explain why she felt such a compulsion to carry on without the villagers' help but she could not resist it, even when the odds were stacked against her. "Let's face it," she continued to justify herself, "*they're* not going to have any effect." She meant the believers in the primeval forces. "Nature wasn't put on this planet for humans to command."

Ryan agreed. "If anything, it's the other way round. But nature wasn't put here for scientists to muck around with either, Jodie. Study, yes. But not muck around with – or it's likely to muck around with us."

230

"I know," Jodie muttered. "That's why we're here. To put a stop to this particular bit of mucking around. So, no more philosophy. Let's concentrate on what we have to do."

"What *are* we going to do?" asked Ryan.

Desperately she said, "We still need a diversion to get us in past the cameras."

The two guards crouched down by the perimeter fence. "What the hell…?"

Immediately, the more nervous partner radioed the office. "We've got ourselves an incursion down here at the stone circle," he reported in an urgent whisper. "God knows what's going on. There's between ten and twenty people. Maybe it's just some wild party. Too dark to tell."

"OK," the orders came back. "Two of you can't do anything. Lay low. I'll send more troops. We need to round them all up. No mistakes. And don't let them see you till we've got enough men there to handle it."

"Understood. Over and out."

His fellow guard giggled softly. "Do you think they're going to strip off and dance naked? I hope so. Count me in!"

"Look," Ryan breathed, pointing to the gatehouse. Several guards had gathered and were milling about outside the Security Office. "Something's going on."

"Let's use it, then," Jodie hissed. "It may be our only chance." She stood up, her face set with determination. "Come on. Are you ready with that paint sprayer? Can you operate it with your fingers crossed?"

Ryan and Wolfie followed her into the ring of light.

The laboratory was a single-storey building with a door at the end. There was a lamp over the entrance and a camera mounted above it. Lurking out of the camera's range, Jodie said, "If we go in from the side, the video won't spot us till we're right at the door. I'll punch in the code as quickly as possible. Just hope that the guards are too occupied to notice us."

Almost immediately, there was a shouted order from the other end of the site and the officers began to filter into the darkness of the grounds.

"In we go !" Jodie whispered.

Jodie went first, cursing the ache in her calf muscle, followed by Wolfie faltering on his bad leg, and Ryan with his black and blue face. As soon as they entered the brilliant envelope of light by the door, they felt extremely vulnerable. With fumbling fingers Jodie tapped 53143 into the combination lock. She was praying that her information was correct, that she wasn't walking into a trap. Her plan could come to an untimely and embarrassing end right here by the door. But when she turned the handle, the door opened with barely a creak. Quickly, she slipped inside and Wolfie and Ryan followed her. They found themselves in a long, dimly lit corridor. She pointed along the passage to where some stairs led down to the basement. Then she laid her forefinger across her lips. Treading softly, Jodie headed for the steps.

Nearer to the flight of stairs, she hesitated. Waiting for Ryan to tiptoe to her side, she pointed upwards. High on the wall at the head of the stair-well, there was a video camera. Jodie wiggled the tip of her forefinger in the air, mimicking the pushing of a button.

Understanding her straightaway, Ryan nodded and sidled forward, keeping out of camera shot until he was almost right underneath it. Then, without hesitating, he put up his arm and sprayed paint from the aerosol can all over the lens. He looked towards Jodie and put up his thumb.

Protected from the video surveillance by a layer of black paint, they trotted downstairs. Wolfie winced and hobbled until he reached the flat surface of the basement corridor.

"On the left," Jodie motioned towards a door some twenty paces away.

They tiptoed down the passageway, lit by pale night-lights. At the door, Jodie opened it a crack and peered inside. No lamps were on so they slipped into the dark interior. Once their eyes were accustomed to the dark, they squinted round the walls for a camera. Ryan found it, betrayed by a small flashing red light on its underbelly, in the far corner. He sprayed it liberally with black paint. "OK," he breathed. "You can turn on the lamp now. If someone's watching the video they'll be none the wiser. They'll think it's still dark."

Flooded with bright light, they took several seconds to blink vision back into their startled eyes. They found themselves in a windowless room. Some sort of small control room. Around the walls, there was a broad white Formica bench, broken only where there was a second door. Under the working surface, there were cupboards. On top, there were computers, printers, monitors, recorders and a television – but no sign of a large RFR generator. Jodie didn't know exactly what the generator would look like but she recognized everything in the room as monitoring and controlling equipment. The device was not on display. While Wolfie sniffed the strange clinical atmosphere, Jodie and Ryan opened each cupboard and glanced inside. Some of them were virtually empty. Others contained connecting cables, obsolete recorders, electronic components, spare motherboards and chips, discs and digital archiving tapes, CD-ROMs.

Straightening up, Jodie said, "Of course! The weapon wouldn't be in here. It's obvious. It would have to be in a screened room – where the RFR pulse can't affect the operators. If they fired it in here they'd stun or kill themselves."

Both of them looked at the other door and made for it instinctively.

A man's lone voice drifted on the wind. "Show us what you need," it droned.

One of the guards shuffled as he lay out on the grass and squinted towards the stone circle. He was still on edge. "What on earth is going on?" he whispered to his colleague.

"No idea. Looks a bit sober for a wild party."

The same voice sounded again. "Show us what you want," it implored.

Suddenly, the first security officer felt something on his outstretched legs. An animal. Believing he was about to be attacked, he yelped in shock and jumped up. The fox took off in one direction and the guard recoiled in the other. In seconds, the officer found himself within the stone circle, surrounded by the pagan worshippers.

The followers of the old ways encircled him and stared menacingly at him. The one who seemed to be the leader exclaimed, "It's the sign." His voice carried threat but also revealed surprise and discomfort.

"What do you mean?" the security officer stammered. "What are you going to do?"

Ignoring the guard, someone else uttered hungrily, "A man. The supreme offering."

"It's the sign," Simon repeated. He breathed deeply, calling up the courage to take the life of a man. Reminding himself that it was only one of the cuckoos, Simon said with more resolve, "It's dangerous but the stones have shown us the way. I have to obey. We have to get rid of the Research Station."

Simon produced a long jagged knife.

What were the pillars of sandstone? To the believers they were a tiny part of the living planet. Not alive but an integral part of the organism like the sensory hairs on an insect. Not just decoration but serving a purpose – sensing their surroundings. The large stone was also like a beacon, able to unleash energy when bidden by humans. To the scientists they were sedimentary rock made of beautiful quartz crystals, compacted and cemented together by a muddy matrix. An elegant network of giant silicon dioxide molecules. Electrons, protons and neutrons arranged ingeniously into atoms in ways that no one fully understood. Wondrous, mysterious particles like quarks and neutrinos that were still being discovered.

If the inanimate stone circle did have a life of its own, it would have been weary of its role as silent witness. Sick of being splashed by the blood of pointless sacrifices. Unresponsive to the petitions of presumptuous human beings. Perhaps once it would have been curious about the ways of men and women, but their entertainment value soon dwindled. Now, if the stone circle had a life, it would probably opt to brush them aside, to wipe those tiresome humans from the face of the earth.

Like a pack of hounds with the smell of blood in the air, the villagers grabbed the struggling guard and began to drag him towards the pitted stone where Simon now waited with the blade. The new Master of the pagans was trembling with fear but his sense of duty outweighed his trepidation. He was bound by the ancient magic to provide the stone circle with the ultimate life energy before he could summon and exploit its might. As Master, Simon had power over life and death. He was beginning to convince himself that it was right to have that power. His fingers gripped even tighter around the knife.

The guard struggled, kicked and screamed but he could not free himself from the masses of villagers who had overpowered him. At the edge of the stone circle, his comrade was shouting out loud for assistance. A short distance away, the approaching band of security officers heard the commotion and, bewildered, charged towards the monument.

The air pressure above the stone circle continued to drop. It sucked in the atmosphere, creating powerful gusts of wind. The sudden gale swirled. Guards mixed chaotically with pagans, staggering, hardly able to keep their feet because of the fierce blasts of wind. The knife flew from Simon's hand or maybe it was knocked. In the confusion, it was hardly possible to distinguish security staff from trespassers. It wasn't one group against another any longer, it was each human against the rushing wind, as strong and irresistible as a torrent of water. In seconds, the potent gale had scattered the whole comical crew.

Jodie grabbed the handle of the RFR laboratory and pulled but the door barley shifted. It was massive and solid, about 15 centimeters thick. Both of them yanked on it to pull it open. Wolfie was the first to enter the screened room, attracted by the smell of animals. There were no live creatures in the laboratory but there were cages and tanks and baskets where they had once been held captive – until they were sacrificed to the research project.

From the edge of the laboratory, Jodie called Wolfie back in a hushed voice. "Just a minute!" She poked her head inside. By the light from the control room, she scrutinized the lab for video surveillance. She knew that the scientists would need a means of viewing the results of their experiments in the room. Somewhere a video camera would be their eyes. A microphone might be their ears as well. Eventually she spotted the camera at the apex of the ceiling above the door. It perched there like an evil, all–seeing owl. She pointed upwards and let Ryan squeeze past her with the aerosol can. After he'd squirted the lens with paint, they walked into the unsettling laboratory. If Jodie hadn't perceived the activities carried out in the suite as a threat to her, to Ryan and Wolfie – and to the world – she would have adored the facilities. An electronic wonderland. But the empty cages reminded her that this was not heaven for physicists but hell for experimental animals. First, she pointed to a microphone resting on one of the Formica tables and again put a finger on her lips. She went to the table and examined the microphone but it seemed to be dead. A wire led from it into a socket in the wall. Jodie put her head back into the control room to see a similar wire emerge from a socket on the other side of the wall. Listening for a reaction from the control room, she returned to the microphone and tapped it. There was no indication of amplified sound from next door so she murmured, "I'm pretty sure it's off and it's just local. Not security. It's so someone in the control room can listen to what's happening in here. I imagine this place is soundproofed and screened with all sorts of things to stop the pulse getting out."

Wolfie continued his exploration of the cages, pushing his nostrils against each one and sampling the scents of dried urine, excrement and blood. The foul smell of petrified animals. A lesser dog would have cowered or turned tail and run, but Wolfie held his proud head high. He was mystified and distressed but he stayed with Jodie and Ryan. He would not abandon his friends.

"I don't know what's going on outside," Jodie whispered, "but it can't be long before they spot three cameras on the blink. It might take them a while to work out they're not bust but sabotaged. When they realize, they'll be down here pretty sharpish. We can't hang about."

"What are we going to do?" Ryan inquired.

Jodie shrugged. "Find the generator and improvize, I suppose."

The sealed room was cold and sinister. On the floor against the walls, there were several transformers and metal cabinets – both big and small – that could house a generator. Jodie strolled past them all, looking for clues, but she could not figure out which were the crucial pieces of equipment. She had no means of recognizing an RFR generator. She tried a different tack. Searching among the tanks and cages, she looked for a means of directing the RFR pulse at the intended target. By one clear plastic tank, she gasped. Held by a clamp attached to a stand, a metallic finger poked down towards the empty tank as if pointing accusingly to a recent atrocity. Jodie stared at it and declared, "This looks like some sort of probe or horn for delivering electromagnetic radiation. I'm sure it's aiming the pulse into the cage," she said excitedly. "It was probably an experiment on mice or rats or something like that."

"If Wolfie could talk," Ryan voiced, "I reckon he'd be able to tell us what was in it – by smell."

Hastily, Jodie began to trace the wire back to find the RFR generator that had to be at the end of it. The wire led her to a small cabinet labelled R402. "This," she inferred, "must be the generator." Peering behind it, she added, "Its power cable's enormous. That figures. It's screened in some way."

"Can't we just pull the plug?" Ryan asked.

"No," answered Jodie. "The cable just disappears into a channel in the wall. I imagine it'll go through to the control room. It'll be operated from there. That's where the on-off switch will be."

"In that case," Ryan murmured, "we're in deep trouble if the guards catch us in here. They can just turn it on and…"

Jodie wasn't listening. With sweat suddenly appearing on her brow, she was examining the unit next to R402. It was called the R402A – obviously an updated model – and it dwarfed the original. It was sitting arrogantly on a sturdy trolley. On top of the cabinet there lay another probe, like the first but enormous. It oozed phenomenal power and peril. It was like being cooped up with a nuclear bomb. Not able to keep the tremor from her voice, she claimed, "I bet this is what they attached to the standing stone when they did the Noah's Ark experiment," she hissed. "It's the mother of all generators and RFR probes."

Ryan joined her. Both of them stared in awe at the two devices. They were scared. They were looking at the next generation of killing machine. They might as well have been standing in front of a loaded gun.

21

Dr Granger clenched the phone between his shoulder and his neck. "At this time of night?" he screeched. "What's going on?" Realizing immediately that he would not be getting an early night after all, he began to button up his shirt again as he spoke.

"I don't know," the Chief of Security replied. "All I know is, I've lost contact with most of my staff. They went to the stone circle to sort out some disturbance and now they're … not responding. It's like they've been whisked away."

Losing his temper, Frank Granger snorted, "Don't talk nonsense. Something's going on, though. That's clear. Send a couple more to take a look. I'm on my way. When I arrive, we'll check internally. I can't see how anyone could get into the buildings – even if we're not a hundred per cent on security measures – but we'll check just in case." He put down the telephone, threw on his jacket and headed for his car.

Jodie looked again at the generators that formed the hearts of the two RFR weapons. "Perhaps the little one – the R402 – is the stun version," she guessed. "The big one's the killer."

"What do we do, then?" Ryan queried. "Any ideas?"

Jodie sucked in air as she thought. There had to be something she could do. But... "Hang on!" she said. "This big one's mobile! And it won't work with a couple of AA batteries, so," she said, moving the trolley to see behind the weapon, "it must work off the mains supply."

She was right. The system had a plug which would fit into a power point in the wall. "Good," she said, suddenly animated. "We can't rip out the R402 but this one we can set up somewhere else."

"Somewhere else? What do you mean?"

"We haven't got time for a chat. Help me push it into the control room. I'll tell you as we go."

The generator was quite a weight. They wheeled it slowly through the doorway. "You see," Jodie explained as they huffed and puffed, "if we did get caught in the RFR lab, we'd be screened from this control room." They stopped the trolley and Jodie looked around. "That cupboard is empty. And there's a power point behind it. Let's put it in there."

"You want us to lift it?" Ryan exclaimed.

"You want to get out of this alive?" Jodie rejoined. "Yes. We've got to." They positioned the trolley alongside the cupboard so that they didn't have to take the weight of the R402A for long. "It works both ways," Jodie added as they steeled themselves. "The screening stops people out here from being exposed to the pulse next door. But…"

"If the pulse is let off out here, we'd be safe in there," Ryan inferred.

"Exactly." Jodie opened the cupboard door, inhaled and asked, "Ready?"

Ryan nodded.

They each tucked their fingers under the edge of the generator and heaved. Groaning, they took the weight. With his foot, Ryan pushed away the trolley and simultaneously with Jodie lowered the device by slowly squatting down. Once they had the R402A in line with the bottom of the cupboard, they moved it sideways. Jodie's arms were aching and leaden. The muscles were tearing and the wound on her left arm was agony. "Can't hold it much longer," she mumbled through gritted teeth.

"Just get one edge on the lip of the cupboard. That'll take the weight. Then we'll push like mad to get it all the way in."

Jodie did not so much place the side of the heavy weapon in the cupboard as drop it. It slammed down with a bang.

Supporting a more manageable proportion of its weight, they adjusted their positions to be along side each other. "OK," Ryan wheezed. "Push!"

Together they strained to shove the generator into the cupboard, like forcing an unwilling cow into a pen. As they struggled, the probe fell off and clattered to the floor. They ignored it. With rapidly approaching exhaustion, they pushed with all their might till the weapon was inside and the door would shut.

They both collapsed on the ground afterwards but Jodie spurred more effort from her tired and throbbing body. She leaned into the cupboard and, uncomfortably close to the murderous apparatus, plugged it into the socket at the back.

Ryan cried in panic, "It won't go off if you turn it on, will it?"

"No," Jodie replied. She flicked on the switch, placed the probe beside the generator in the cupboard, and explained, "I've just powered it up. It'll be in a standby mode, probably charging up ready for action. That's if I didn't break it when I dropped it – and the probe. Anyway, as long as it still works, it'll only fire a pulse when it receives the start signal. So," she said, looking around, "I need to plug in a remote control wire so it can be told to go off." She spun twice on the spot, looking lost. Exasperated, she spread her arms. "I haven't got a clue what the lead's like and what to connect it to!"

Ryan was also stumped. He stared at the door to the corridor as if the guards were about to burst in. He did not dare to open it and put his head outside to check for activity.

Frustrated, Jodie muttered, "What do we do? What do we do?"

Ryan sighed. Resigned to failure, he said, "Oh, well. It's wrong to let it off in here anyway. We'd kill whoever was round. I promised Mum we wouldn't get involved in violence. And remember what Dad said to you about revenge."

"This isn't revenge," Jodie retorted. "It's about stopping a weapon – protecting ourselves. That's it!" she cried. "I know."

"What?" Ryan enquired, following her back into the inner laboratory.

"The answer's in here," Jodie said, as she examined the original R402. "The other model's the same as this – just its big brother. So, I can take the control lead from this one and put it on the R402A. If the guards catch us in here – they're bound to soon – and decide to push the button to stun us, they'll fire the R402A instead, unbeknown to them. They'll nobble themselves, not us. We'll be safe in here. That's not us being violent, Ryan. It's them. They'll only hurt themselves if they try to hurt us."

Hardly pausing, she mumbled, "The trouble is, this control lead is moulded into place! I can't take it off." She muttered a curse. "That means I can't use it for the other weapon! But at least I know what one looks like now, what to look for."

"This?" Ryan asked. He grasped a cable lying on the floor where the trolley had been.

"Yes! That's it," Jodie cried, congratulating him and taking it from him. "You get the trolley back in here. Luckily, without video, they won't be able to see the generator's gone. I'll go and see where I have to plug this in."

Jodie traced the wire from the R402 to a control box attached to the wall. On the other side, in the control room, there was an identical box. The wire continued from the box into a console on the white bench below. Undoubtedly, now the computers were out of action, the weapon would be operated from this unit. But none of the cables leading to the R402 ended in a plug. The wire was moulded into each junction box. Jodie could not detach it. She could not disable the R402.

But she *could* enable the mobile weapon. She could attach its control cable to the console alongside the connection to the R402. There was a socket under the console and it was the right size for the plug on the wire in her hand. She ran the cable along the floor to the cupboard where they had secreted the R402A.

Watching her plug it into the larger generator, Ryan said, "Won't they see the wire by the wall and know we've done something?"

"Possibly," Jodie replied. "We'll just have to hope they're too busy with us to see it. It's not that obvious. It just looks it to you because you know it's there."

Interrupting her, Ryan whispered urgently, "I hear something. Sounds like someone on the stairs. I think they're coming!"

Wincing at the pain in her arm and leg, Jodie scrambled to her feet. "Well, I think it's set up. If they try and zap us, we're stuck. I can't do anything about it, I'm afraid. We'll be stunned again. Not pleasant. But I've made sure they'll zap themselves as well."

They retreated to the inner laboratory and pretended to pore over the RFR probe as if they'd just found the operations room and broken in. As they waited in the dungeon-like laboratory to discover their fate, Ryan whispered, "I wouldn't say I'm feeling brave about this, Jodie. I'm terrified."

Jodie touched his arm. She was about to open her mouth when someone crashed through the outer door.

There was still no news of the mysterious events at the stone circle. The extra two guards had found nothing at all. The Director met his security chief in the video surveillance room. While the operation at the stone circle was in progress, there were not enough officers to staff the monitors. On such a crazy night, the Chief had looked them over whenever he could. Straightaway, Frank pointed to the screens that were monitoring the RFR lab and its inner sanctum. "Blank," he grunted, frowning.

"No problem," the Head replied. "Been like that for a while. No lights on, that's all."

"What about the stairs?" Frank roared. "The night lights are always on!"

The screen was as black as ink.

"The camera might be on the blink."

"At the same time as a dodgy midnight invasion of the grounds? You've got to be joking! It was a cover. Someone's broken in. Come on!"

Dr Granger ran from the room with his Head of Security in tow. Fighting against a ridiculous wind that tore at their faces and clothes, they dashed across the compound to the laboratory building. Punching in the code, they stepped into the calm of the Physics Block. Down the corridor, they paused at the top of the stairs and the Security Officer looked up at the camera. "Paint!" he snarled.

They scurried down the stairs to the laboratory entrance. Frank Granger was in front when they reached the door and he opened it so that his Head of Security could go in first. He wanted someone else to establish that it was safe before he entered.

Without hesitating, the chief thrust himself through the door. "No one here!" he exclaimed.

But at the door to the RFR laboratory itself, a wolfhound appeared and barked viciously.

Dr Granger smiled evilly and, above the dog's racket, ordered, "Slam the door shut. Then we've got them."

The security officer looked at the Director and then at the growling dog. He was wondering which was more malicious. Deciding he'd rather take on a wolfhound than his boss, he edged towards the massive door, hoping that the dog would not suddenly attack him. He was lucky. The wolfhound, one of his front legs heavily bandaged, growled threateningly but was not in a fit state to go on the offensive. When the guard put his shoulder to the door and pushed it closed, the dog backed away. The Head of Security caught sight of two young intruders, a boy and a girl, before the door shut and sealed with a satisfying click and a hiss.

"Good," Frank Granger announced with a satisfied smile. "I think we've just about got this wrapped up."

He strolled to the monitor and his fingers stretched out for a switch. "Let's get it over with," he snorted. He flicked the switch. It was marked *Door lock* and a clunk sounded in the heavy door. His finger hovered over a green button and he hesitated for a moment. Then he made up his mind and pressed it. As soon as he took his finger off the *Sound on* button, a faint background hum pervaded the room. "Well," he said aloud, "what have we here? You can speak normally and I'll hear you. Who are you? Or should I guess?"

The detached female voice declared, "Who are you? Dr Granger?"

"Yes," the Director replied. "As you seem to be in a guessing mood, I assume you're Jodie Hilliard, the computer whiz-kid."

"And a boy," the Head of Security put in.

"Ryan Aplin," a young man's tone admitted.

"A bold plot," Dr Granger observed like a smarmy conqueror, magnanimous to his victims. "You got in. No doubt you wanted to steal our RFR weapon. And you got this far. Not bad. But it was a big mistake. You won't get any further. You're in there with the weapon and I can fire it any time I want to. You'll not see the light of day again."

For a couple of seconds, his easy prey did not reply. Then Jodie said, "Are you saying you can kill with this R402 device? It's not just a stun version?"

"It's not our biggest system but it doesn't have to be to swamp a small laboratory. Of course it kills. I just need to select the right parameters from out here. Boost the amplitude and you're dead on demand."

The dismembered quaking voice responded, "I wouldn't do that if I were you."

Dr Granger laughed. "What's this? A threat?" He was amused.

There was a pause and a few mumbled words that he could not make out. Then, eventually, Jodie answered, "Sort of. You see, just in case, this afternoon I wrote a report on everything I know about what you're doing here. I've set my computer to E-mail it automatically to every newspaper I could find on the Internet. It'll be sent out before morning. Of course, I can stop it, but only if I get out of this alive."

Dr Granger's eyebrows rose. He turned off the microphone and said to his security chief, "When we're done here, get a man over to Hilliard's place and destroy her computer. Then it won't send anything ever again." Turning the sound system back on, he admitted, "You're a resourceful young lady, Jodie. Pity all your efforts are pointless and wayward. You give me no choice but to remove you."

"Like you removed Dad?"

"Precisely."

"You did all the killing behind his back, didn't you? Till you murdered him with it."

"It was easy," Dr Granger sniggered. "Like the other physicists as well, he didn't *really* want to know. They believed in the pursuit of knowledge but not its application. Head-in-the-clouds idealists, all of them. Pathetic."

"There's something else you should know," Jodie stammered.

Ignoring some strange background noises, the Director snapped, "No more, please! I don't want to hear any more bluffs. I can understand your delaying tactics but it's getting tedious." His palm rested gently on the large red switch marked *Fire* and, underneath in big letters, *Danger*. "This," he said to himself pleasurably, "will end the whole sorry saga for good." He leaned heavily on the button.

22

"You'll not see the light of day again," said the unseen Director.

Jodie's mouth opened but, for a while, she couldn't speak. It had all started to go wrong. She had assumed that the smaller weapon would only stun while the bigger version was used for killing. She was prepared to be stunned, but she wasn't ready to be sacrificed for an electronic weapon. To make sure, she asked, "Are you saying you can kill with this R402 device? It's not just a stun version?"

Dr Granger's ghostly reply chilled her. It confirmed her miscalculation. "It's not our biggest system but it doesn't have to be to swamp a small laboratory. Of course it kills. I just need to select the right parameters from out here. Boost the amplitude and you're dead on demand."

Ryan and Jodie stared at each other. They both realized that they were about to die. They froze. It was almost impossible to move, hard to think. But neither of them were ready to accept the inevitable. They were fighters. They had not come through the last few awful days to give up now. Jodie demanded that her brain come back on line. She would not play the part of a dumb animal in the savage hands of a pagan worshipper. She searched for a means of making Frank Granger think again. There had to be a way. Trying to control her voice that seemed to want to go up two octaves, she said aloud, "I wouldn't do that if I were you."

The Director's chuckle echoed around them like a mischievous spirit. "What's this?" he bellowed. "A threat?"

Into Ryan's mind came a picture of Dr Hilliard's slippers. He recalled what Wolfie had done to them. The dog's strong teeth and jaws had ripped and torn and pulped them. Ryan clutched the wire from the RFR probe and forced his tense body to kneel down. He showed the cable to Wolfie, putting it right up to his nose, and looked up at Jodie. She realized what Ryan had in mind and nodded briskly. Wolfie sniffed at it and looked quizzically at Ryan.

To Jodie, Ryan breathed, "Keep him talking." Then he returned to the task in hand. To show Wolfie what he had to do, Ryan took the substantial cable in his own mouth and mimicked a chewing action.

Wolfie's expressive face showed surprise. When he was presented with the wire again, he sniffed once more and licked it.

Ryan shook his head in desperation. He shoved it into his mouth again and chewed on the unyielding insulation.

Suddenly, Wolfie got the idea. His face almost beamed. He'd been given permission to sharpen his teeth on something that he'd normally be chastized for wrecking. He set about the task with gusto.

"Sort of," Jodie began. "You see, just in case, this afternoon I wrote a report on everything I know about what you're doing here. I've set my computer to E-mail it automatically to every newspaper I could find on the Internet. It'll be sent out before morning. Of course, I can stop it, but only if I get out of this alive." Jodie was lying. She'd written a report, but she'd already mailed it. Nightshift reporters were probably already on their way.

The hum in the room ceased for a while. Jodie guessed that Dr Granger had turned off the sound to talk to his colleague in private. Looking at Wolfie, she said, "Good boy. Keep going."

As Wolfie bit it, the plastic coating scrunched pleasingly on his teeth. He could feel the plastic become pliable as he used the power in his jaws to soften it. He settled on the floor and shifted the cable to his molars where it squeaked satisfyingly. With his back teeth he could really get to work –

gnawing, crushing, grinding. He hesitated when two things happened at once. His teeth contacted something hard. Metal. And he was interrupted by the voice of the man that he could not see. He let the cable hang loose from his slobbering mouth.

"You're a resourceful young lady, Jodie. Pity all your efforts are pointless and wayward. You give me no choice but to remove you."

Whispering right into Wolfie's ear, Ryan encouraged him, "You've got to keep going. Please!" Urgently, he added, "If you want to live, if you want Jodie to live, keep chewing!"

Wolfie seemed to respond to Ryan's vehemence and passion. He seemed to realize that it was important to bite through the cable, even if there was something rigid, steely and unpleasant in it.

Playing for time as best she could, Jodie asked, "Like you removed Dad?"

His reply was God-like. "Precisely." This was a man who thought that he had power over life and death. Of course, he did. But he also seemed to believe that it was right to have that power.

"You did all the killing behind his back, didn't you? Till you murdered him with it."

Wolfie winced as his teeth continued to grate on the resilient wire.

Frank Granger could not keep the humour from his voice. "It was easy," he claimed. "Like the other physicists as well, he didn't *really* want to know.

They believed in the pursuit of knowledge but not its application. Head-in-the-clouds idealists, all of them. Pathetic."

Trying to maintain the exchange with the deranged Director of the Research Station, Jodie stammered, "There's something else you should know."

In Wolfie's throat, a low growl formed as he persuaded himself that he was angry with the cable. He took it in his front teeth and shook his head with such violence that the remaining plastic tore away and even the metal wire began to shred.

Dr Granger butted in. "No more, please!" he wailed theatrically. "I don't want to hear any more bluffs. I can understand your delaying tactics but it's getting tedious."

Ryan and Jodie exhorted Wolfie, "More! Now, Wolfie. Give it all you've got!"

Wolfie didn't want to let down the girl who had been so good to him. Not after all she'd done. He wanted to please her. He slapped a great big paw on the cable, pinning it to the ground. He clamped his teeth firmly on the part that he had chewed. Then he jerked his head ferociously in the opposite direction. Almost immediately, he yelped with pain and blood spurted from the loose flesh of his jaw as the bare wire ripped right through it. He jumped back, bewildered and hurt. But the cable dropped out of his injured mouth in two pieces.

Wolfie had broken the circuit.

*   *   *

Dr Granger leaned hard on the button and almost instantaneously felt something grip his brain. An RFR pulse saturated the building. For a second, his whole body became agonizingly stiff. His head felt as if it would explode. Behind him the Head of Security collapsed to the floor with a thud. Granger was not so lucky. He lived for a few seconds longer. He felt himself lose control of all bodily functions and he heard his heart pound so violently that it seemed to burst with excruciating pain in his chest. Then his brain released him. He slithered to the floor. As he fell, his right hand caught the *Door lock* switch and released it. At the same time the RFR pulse released him from life. His body thumped sickeningly and clumsily on the floor. His head cracked unpleasantly on the hard surface and a trickle of blood appeared like a perverse halo. Humanity had deserted him as soon as he'd hit the button. Now the room was devoid of human life.

23

Apart from the quiet hum, there hadn't been a sound from the speaker for at least two minutes. Jodie was comforting and congratulating Wolfie. "You saved us! And you've got war wounds to prove it. I'm sorry. It's back to a vet for you, my lad." She was relieved but worried for Wolfie.

"Do you think it's safe to go out?" Ryan asked, still suspicious.

Jodie nodded. "It's deadly quiet. I think Granger pulled the trigger. But the pulse doesn't last. It does its damage in a second or two, then it's gone. Just like that. It'll be safe."

Together they pushed open the door. Immediately, Jodie put her hand over her mouth. "Ugh!"

Ryan looked away from the two bodies. He put

his arm around Jodie's shoulders and guided her past the carnage and out of the door. Wolfie followed, hobbling even more than he did before and dripping blood from his cut mouth. He didn't even stop to sniff the dead.

Out in the passageway, Jodie took one look at the steps and said, "Wolfie won't make it up there. There's got to be a lift somewhere. They must have got all the gear down here in one. Let's try the other way."

They didn't worry about the cameras in the corridor now. They didn't care any more. It was all over.

Outside the lift, there lay a guard. He too was dead. When the lift arrived and its doors sprang apart invitingly, Jodie, Ryan and Wolfie stepped round him to go in. Upstairs, they saw two more bodies littering the building. Jodie murmured gloomily, "I wonder how far the effect got."

The lethal RFR pulse had penetrated beyond the walls of the block. Outside, there was a dead crow by the door. "Probably sitting on the roof when it went off," Ryan suggested.

Jodie nodded. "I hope it wasn't just flying past because that'd mean the pulse went a long long way."

But they saw no other evidence of the release of the weapon. It had been contained almost entirely within the building.

The only guard left in the Security Office was unharmed but confused and unsure of himself. Video pictures from the physics section were showing some of his fallen colleagues. His chief was not answering his radio-phone and the Director's mobile telephone rang and rang. The lone officer had to believe the horrifying incident that Jodie and Ryan related. When Jodie insisted that he should call in the police, he was too despondent to argue. The Research Station was finished. This one was too big to cover up. The truth about the victims of the RFR weapon was about to be revealed. Scandal and closure awaited the laboratory.

Jodie hardly recognized her grandad. He looked older and more decrepit than his years. His life and health had been shattered when his only daughter had died. Jodie's grandma was too ill to undertake the long journey. Clearly, the Australian outback had not been able to fix what was broken beyond repair. Jodie had every sympathy for her grandparents but she became even more convinced that her future did not reside with them. They were too distant emotionally, in age and outlook. And they were too distant from Jodie's roots.

Yes, Jodie wanted a new beginning. But, to start afresh, she didn't need a new alien home miles from Alice Springs on the other side of the planet. She needed understanding. She needed Ryan. With the

Research Station's activities exposed, Jodie and Ryan could begin to fill the holes that their fathers had left in their lives. They could do it best together. They wanted to share the problems that would challenge them. Mrs Aplin was too devastated to agree to becoming Jodie's guardian. Every time she looked at Jodie, she would have been reminded of her husband's murder. Besides, once she'd made a complete recovery from her physical wounds, Mrs Aplin intended to return to Scotland and live with her sister. Ryan had the freedom and the right to make his own choices. He chose to be with Jodie, whatever she did. Wolfie added his voice to the chorus. He risked the stitches in the side of his mouth by barking inexhaustibly at Jodie's grandfather.

It was at the funerals that the issue resolved itself. This time, the Hell Fire Club really did come to Jodie's rescue. Mr and Mrs Jackson, Leah's parents, were distraught about their daughter but they also recognized Jodie's plight. Jodie had been their daughter's wronged friend, she had uncovered the truth about Leah's death and she had risked everything to put it to rights. They were not prepared to see her whisked away against her wishes because she fell short of her eighteenth birthday by four months. They offered to become her legal guardians. It was with relief that Jodie's grandad consented and set off for home.

The police file on Simon, fourteen other villagers and ten guards remained open. Missing persons. No one would ever know what happened on that dreadful night. The earth seemed to have swallowed the lot of them. Perhaps it had. Then, it was the earth itself that provided Jodie and Ryan with the decoy they needed to put an end to the weapon. It was the earth that arranged for the stone circle to be cleansed of both pagan and scientific interference. The earth had used Jodie and Ryan for its own purpose.

In the village, the small urns were removed from The Olde Spotted Dog and destroyed. Another room in the pub was opened to the public. The future inhabitants of Greenwood End confined their calls for regeneration to street festivities.

Beyond the still beechwood, the stones rested in blissful silence.

At sunset, the massive sandstone rock glowed deep red. Over the centuries. it had been scarred and furrowed by lightning and rain. To the Aborigines of central Australia, the gigantic rock was sacred – the source of their strength – but this evening, it served a different purpose. Without even a hint of wind, the summer air was oppressively warm and stale. In the scrubland, the stunted trees and shrubs were as motionless at statues of the dead. Even the cicadas had ceased their rasping.

One creature did slink noiselessly towards the brooding rock. Its eyes glinted faintly as it moved its head from side to side, gazing stealthily over the plain. It paused and hung its nose in the air to catch an intriguing scent. Suddenly, the animal froze, its tongue lolled and saliva dripped from its hungry mouth. It had detected the sheep and rabbits that were tethered helplessly in front of the giant sandstone and shifting restlessly as if they sensed the danger. With its broad muzzle, bushy tail and short brown coat, the wolf-like dingo began to prowl towards its prey, fixing its stare on one particular lamb.

The lamb lifted its face and surveyed the territory. It tilted its head quizzically and bleated twice. It did not see the predator but it knew that there was something out there. It backed away. The tether drew taut.

Sneaking within a few metres of the helpless lamb, the dingo suddenly sprang forward. In mid-flight, though, it pulled up. It was distracted by something that it could not see, smell, hear or feel. It stared in panic at the rock, cowered, then turned tail and, yelping, ran away across the grassland at speed, leaving behind its easy prey.

The night reeked of evil.